# Should It Happen To A Barmaid?

The stories are based loosely on real events but all characters are fictitious.

Although the author and publisher have made every effort to ensure that the information in this book was correct at press time, the author and publisher do not assume and hereby disclaim any liability to any party for any loss, damage, or disruption caused by errors or omissions result from negligence, accident, or any other cause.

Published 2015 by Donna Harris Publishing

© Donna Harris 2015

ISBN: 978-09931802-2-4

Printed by Short Run Press

The moral right of the author has been asserted

*Dedication*

For a true friend who has inspired me to write this book
and has given me the confidence to do so.

# Acknowledgements

My thanks go to all friends encouraging me to write, and to all who have contributed their ideas for this book. My special thanks go to Paul for the cover photos, Phil and Nicky for providing the location, and the team at Short Run Press for their help and production of the finished product.

# Should It Happen To A Barmaid?

## *One*

Gemma was running late for work, she needed to be at the pub by 7pm, fortunately the pub where she worked, The Modbury Inn, was only a five minute walk away. It was already 6.55pm, checking she had her keys on her; Gemma closed her house door and swiftly walked up the hill.

Colin, the landlord was heading off to a drinks party nearby. He rarely left the pub, but knew he could leave Gemma in charge for a few hours. Gemma's shift on a busy Friday evening is normally seven until ten, but often when the bar quiets down; Colin will let her clock off early. She had agreed to stay until Colin returned.

Gemma enjoyed her shifts at the pub. Friday evenings were often fun. With people unwinding after a busy week of work, with the anticipation of a couple of days off for the weekend, there was usually a jolly atmosphere. The pub attracted a lot of men. There were the early drinking crowd, normally six until seven. They were the older gentlemen, who enjoyed testing their knowledge on the crossword that appeared in the daily paper. Bill, a retired teacher, would read out the questions. The banter would fly, with the answers flying back at him. He was a natural schoolmaster. They would finally find the correct answers to fit the questions, and if they didn't they would then review their mistakes at their next gathering.

The younger working chaps would generally flock in the pub at around seven, having possibly made a stop somewhere en route home. The lads would often have a game of spoof for their drinks, by guessing how many coins are in their individual hand, resulting in a knock out guessing game, where the looser buys the round of drinks. Gemma had a full time day job working as a marketing assistant. Having recently gone through an upsetting divorce, she found the easiest way to socialise was to work as a barmaid in the local pub. She had known many of the locals for many years, and felt comfortable in their company, and could laugh with them at their banter. Gemma also fitted the bill as an attractive barmaid. Medium height, curvaceous figure, light coloured hair, blue eyes and a size 36 double D chest. Her bubbly cheeky nature also gave her the right credentials for the job. She enjoyed the flirtatious banter, and felt safe with the bar between herself and the customers.

Barmaids are very much 'on show' with people queuing for their drinks with their eyes peeled at them. It is the same for both sexes. Studying the person pulling your pint or pouring the vino, checking them out from head to toe is normal practice in most bars. It is not a job for the terribly shy, or anyone who is a bad communicator, as a good bar person is known to be a credit to the team.

"We are off now." Colin explained to Gemma.

"I have checked the barrels, you should be ok, and Tom is always here to help if you do need a barrel changing. We are not far away, do ring if you need us."

Gemma had been left in charge of the bar before, and had coped well. If the bar did get busy, then Tom being one of the locals, would always step in and help pull a pint if necessary. The kitchen staff looked after the food orders, which left Gemma free to look after the bar.

"I will be fine." replied Gemma "You go and have fun."

It was late May and daylight until around ten. Gemma knew the pub would be quiet, with many drinkers having headed home early to enjoy the good weather and light evenings with their families. With only about six people in the bar, she thought it would be a fairly un eventful evening.
Bill took the last gulp out of his glass.

"I am off now Gemma, and heading down the road for a drink at Annabel's before going home for tea."

Bill lived in the town, and being a creature of habit, he always ended his week with a short walk up the hill to the Modders for a couple of pints whilst completing the crossword. He then headed downtown for a Guinness with Annabel at the Bistro.

"Bye Bill, see you next week when I am in next." smiled Gemma

There were a few lads playing spoof by the bar, and apart from a few people dining, all was quiet. Gemma busied herself by cleaning some glasses from the earlier drinkers, and wiping the beer spillage from the tables. There was a long mirror at the back of the bar, and as she walked behind carrying some glasses, she noticed a gentlemen walk into the pub. Gemma turned and immediately blushed, as she had noticed in the mirror that he was a very good looking chap.

*Oh My!* She thought, and beamed a smile.

"What can I get you?" Gemma asked

"Half a pint of larger shandy please." came the reply. Gemma was almost stage struck. She managed to pour the drink and asked the gentleman for his money.

"That will be £1.60 please."

Gemma took his cash, and turned to the till and let out a little "Phew" whilst thinking *'he is hot!*

The gentleman was wearing a dark grey suit, a white shirt, but no tie. With his shirt open, she could see he had a very nice tan. *Maybe a Solicitor or an Accountant?* Gemma thought. She turned back to face him with his change. He thanked her, smiled, and took the corner seat in the bar. Gemma turned to serve another customer; she couldn't help thinking how good looking the stranger was. *Maybe he is new in town she thought?* He didn't seem to know anyone else. Then maybe he was just passing through, as many businessmen often did.
He didn't seem in a hurry to drink his Shandy.

Gemma could see he was checking her out too. She was disappointed when another couple of customers came through the door, as she couldn't get to chat to the stranger.

After about half an hour, Gemma noticed that he had finished his drink. *Oh no, she thought, is he about to leave?* She hadn't had time to flirt with him, let alone find anything out about him.
To her delight, he asked for another drink.

"May I have another please?"

"Same again?" Gemma inquired

"Yes please" he replied

Again she couldn't help but notice how incredibly good looking he was. With jet black spikey hair, and a hint of designer stubble. What she could see of his physique under his jacket, he did look rather fit.

This time, when Gemma handed him his change, she plucked up the courage to ask "Are you new to the area, or just passing through?"

He smiled. "Moved into Kingston a few weeks ago. On my way back from Plymouth, so I thought I would check out Modbury. My name is Steve."

He wasn't in a hurry to drink up, and in between serving a few more customers, Gemma was able to enjoy some quality flirting time.

"What time do you finish work?" he asked

"Around nine, once the landlord's back." Gemma replied.

"I am not in a hurry; I will buy you a drink if you like? You can tell me a bit more about the area."

*How exciting Gemma thought, that would be a real treat.*

"Ok, that would be nice; the Landlord should be back soon."

Gemma couldn't contain her excitement, and her mood was bubbling.
It wasn't too long before Colin the landlord returned, and as he walked in he noticed the stranger in the corner. Gemma introduced them.

"Hi Colin, hope you enjoyed the drinks party? This is Steve; he is new to the area and has just moved to Kingston."

Colin shook Steve's hand. He always had time for new customers. Colin knew by looking at Steve that Gemma would be smitten.

"You can clock off now if you like Gemma." Steve ordered a glass of Pinot for Gemma, and an Orange juice for himself.

They moved into the lounge, where it was quieter for them to chat. Gemma was able to find out more about Steve.

"What do you do for a living?" Gemma enquired.

"I am a financial advisor, working mainly from home."

They immediately hit it off. Enjoying flirting with each other, there was no shortage of conversation. Gemma knew the area well, and recommended several places for Steve to visit. She was in her element. He was the first person that had really caught her attention since her divorce. She had been married for six years, but had never had children. She had free time in the evenings, and had nothing to rush home for.

Gemma was disappointed when Steve explained that he was married. Although the marriage was not a happy one, else he wouldn't be chatting her up she thought. She was not looking for an affair, but was looking for a distraction to get her over the divorce. Maybe the wine had started to have an effect on her; she had not eaten before leaving home and turning up for her bar shift.

"How would you like to come back to my place for some bubbles and a dip in the hot tub?" Steve asked.

At first Gemma declined the invitation. But then as Steve was about to leave, she accepted his offer. Steve looked an honourable chap she thought. She had been taken in by his dashing good looks and she was smitten.

"I will drive you." Steve said

Kingston was only a ten minute drive, and it wasn't the end of the world if the evening went wrong and she had to walk back. She knew the route well. Steve's wife was away on a girly holiday, and was not due back until Sunday.

Gemma let Colin know where she was going. "Be careful, he looks a nice enough chap, but you never know, he looks the type that could break your heart."

Steve had gone to collect his car, an Audi, and picked Gemma up outside the pub. Gemma's heart was pounding and she had butterflies in her stomach. She had been having a torrid time through the breakup of her marriage. Having never experienced a hot tub before, she had no idea what to expect.

Once at the house, Steve grabbed some towels and handed one to Gemma. He then chose a bottle of chilled champagne out of the fridge and led her to the patio where the hot tub was situated. He turned on the controls and went off to change. There was a music system close to the doors of the patio area, and Gemma put on an Ellie Golding CD Halcyon Days.

Steve appeared back with the towel around his waist. Gemma noticed his fit physique; his chest was smooth other than a few dark random hairs growing centrally on him. Gemma felt shy, but on seeing him slip off his towel and step into the tub, her eyes were treated to a feast of his masculinity, she was soon keen to follow.

"Come on don't be shy, it's lovely and warm." Steve was smiling

He was sat with his back to the edge of the tub, arms stretched out invitingly.
Gemma treated him to slowly undressing whilst he watched her, revealing her curvaceous body.

Although it was dark, he was able to see enough with the light reflexion from the hot tub. Gemma enjoyed the look of pleasure in Steve's eyes, as she lowered herself into the tub. He handed her a glass of champagne and they toasted the evening. They chatted for a while. Steve had his arm around Gemma's shoulders as they sat side by side. Gemma turned to face him, and they kissed. Gemma was turned on by the atmosphere, the warmth of the water, the power of the jets, the champagne, and by Steve, with his jet black hair.

Steve was turned on too. He was teasing her by trickling champagne over her body as he kissed his way around her curves.

Gemma pulled away for a minute. What was she doing? She had never taken off with a random stranger before. Especially a married one. Could she be strong enough not to be hurt? She didn't want to be a stepping stone whilst his marriage was failing. But oh my, she was in heaven. He could sense she was hesitant.

"Don't worry, we can stop now if you like, up to you?" Steve was a gentleman.

Gemma placed her glass down and turned back to face Steve. He took a mouthful of his champagne and kissed her. Whilst sharing the fizz which powered into her mouth. It was magic. What a feeling, she was momentarily lost, the track which was playing on the Ellie Golding CD was Explosion. It added to the seduction of the moment. Gemma melted, she sat across him and let him inside her. Steve gave her a level of passion that she had never experienced before, and one which she would never forget.

# Should It Happen To A Barmaid?

## *Two*

The Cheltenham Festival, held in March each year, is a popular pilgrimage for thousands of race goers. Set in the stunning location of Prestbury Park, near Cheltenham town centre in Gloucestershire, it is the stage for four days of classic horse steeplechase and hurdling races. People flock from far and wide, with the town a buzz and a sell out with local accommodation.

Some racegoers choose to book into accommodation within a few miles of the race course, taking either a direct train route, or taxis to the event. With the huge number of visitors to the area, there is also a high demand for casual staff to help with the extra workload of visitors.

Gemma was keen on racing, and also enjoyed the atmosphere of the event, which attracted a predominantly male following. She was able to spend a few days racing, together with taking on some casual evening work at one of the local hotels, The Holiday Inn. Gemma worked on a rota with other lasses who would also take on casual work during the Cheltenham Festival.

The Holiday Inn is situated on the edge of town within walking distance of the train station. There would be plenty of chaps choosing the hotel due to its location. The chaps would travel from wide and far, some as far as Ireland, some just throughout England. Their parties would start once they had joined the train from their home location, carrying on through the days racing events and well into the early hours of the morning.

Gemma's shift started at 9am until 12 noon, just giving her time enough to get to the racecourse for the first race. She then took the later shift; in this case it was 8pm until 2am. It proved a few long days, but if it was a way for her to see some racing, enjoy the atmosphere, and fund her few days away, then she kept going on adrenaline.

The public were arriving  thick and fast in the morning. Check in time wasn't until 3pm onwards, but there would often be groups wanting to get checked in and change before heading to the track. They would be allowed to leave their bags in the locker with a view to check in later in the day.

Geoff had travelled up from Devon with his brother Jack, and their friend Harry. They had booked a room for the three of them, and like many others had been having a drink or two on the train ride up. They were all in good spirits, and bounced up to the reception desk.

"We can't let you have access to the room until after 3pm." Gemma was prepared for the question that Geoff was about to ask her.

"That's a shame, but we are dressed ready, can we leave our bags please?"

Geoff flirted and smiled at Gemma, he noticed that she was a very pretty girl and of an Eastern European nationality.

"No problem, I will label your bags and lock them in the

store room." replied Gemma.

It was about 10.30am and Gemma too was keen to get everyone looked after as soon as possible, so she could get to the races.

The chaps, all in their mid-fifties thanked her and headed off in the direction of the race course. The first day of the Cheltenham Festival was electric. The anticipation of all the waiting for some of the most talented horses to compete for the top National Hunt titles. It's a fabulous sporting experience for all involved in the racing industry. Geoff, his brother Jack and Harry were having a fantastic day. Jack was having most of the betting luck, with the other two struggling to back the winners. Jack however, had won a large sum of money, and decided to spoil the other two with unlimited drinks.

Gemma had also had a great day at the races; she was keen on racing and rode out at a local racing yard. They had given her a day ticket to get in. Later in the week she had planned to meet up with friends and enjoy the festival too. But for now, she headed back to the hotel to start her evening shift at 8pm. Many of the people had already checked in, but Gemma noticed that Geoff and his mates were still yet to collect their bags and take their room. The bar was buzzing with many well sozzled after the first exciting day. Gemma covered both the reception and the bar.

Geoff's crowd turned up around 10pm, they had stopped off in one of the local restaurants for supper before heading back to the hotel. They turned up at the bar for a nightcap.

"Have you had a lucky day?" Gemma asked.

"Jack was very lucky, he put £100 on a 20-1 outsider, so drinks are on him tonight." beamed Geoff.

"Can you give me some tips Jack please? I only have a small flutter now and again, but a winner like that would be great." chuckled Gemma

Geoff was getting very tipsy and enjoyed flirting with Gemma who was in her early twenties, over thirty years younger than him.
Gemma could see that the chaps were ready to crash out in their rooms, so showed them to the store where they had left their bags earlier, and took them up to their room which was on the first floor of the hotel.

"Good night chaps, breakfast is at 7am until 9am."

The men were chatting away and thanked her. They were very pleased to be able to crash out. Geoff undressed and passed out on the bed. He didn't have time to put on his pyjamas, with the hotel heating still on in March, he stripped off his underpants with his trousers. Jack and Harry just laughed and left him to it.

Geoff awoke about midnight needing a wee. He was still a little drunk at the time, but managed to make it to what he thought was the toilet door. He went through the door and into what he thought was the toilet. The door shut behind him. Ooops he thought, this isn't the loo. He had in fact walked into the corridor of the hotel. Realising his mistake, and quickly sobering up noticing he was naked, he hammered on the door to wake the boys. But all he could hear was snoring. *What an earth would he do now he thought?*

Holding his hands over his nether regions, to hide his embarrassment, he headed down the corridor. He also noticed to his horror, that the hall was one long window along the length of the hallway. Being on the first floor, he had been stark naked to all outside, the car park, the road, the visitors arriving late, all of them. He ran down the corridor and found the stairs. He was too embarrassed to use the lift, in case he shocked anyone greeting him the other end. He headed down the stairs to find the reception and bar, still holding onto his dignity. He passed by the toilets and looked in for a towel, but couldn't find anything suitable.
Still covering his nether regions, Geoff walked shyly up to the reception, where he was greeted by Gemma smiling.

"I am really sorry, but I have locked myself out of my room!"

Gemma was trying to contain her amusement.

"No problem, what was your room number?"

"I can't remember?" Geoff replied

Gemma could see he was embarrassed. She handed him the visitor's book to use as a cover to hold over his front.

"What name is the room booked under?"
"I am not sure of that either?"

Geoff can remember his brother teasing the receptionist with the name booking, as his name is similar to a celebratory. Or maybe it was Jack's name the room was booked under.

Gemma stayed calm. Ah I have found it now; I will show you to your room.
Geoff was even more embarrassed. He had made a right fool of himself in front of this beautiful young lady he had been flirting with in the bar earlier in the evening. Gemma led him up to his room, passed the long window again, and opened the door to his room.

"There you are, is there anything else I can help you with?" asked Gemma.
*If only, he thought*!

The boys were too embarrassed to stop for breakfast in the morning, and headed back off to the races for another day of fun.

# Should It Happen To A Barmaid?

## *Three*

Gemma had taken some bar work at the local country castle where wedding parties and functions are held in the beautiful parkland setting. With a lake running through the valley, sloping banks either side and up the hill to a level area of about two acres, is situated the permanent fixture of a grand marquee.

During the winter months, the venue is used for large shooting parties, with banquet lunches served after a busy morning's shoot. The shoot would finish around 1pm, after which the gamekeepers would tend to the dogs which had been working hard, flushing out the pheasants, which had been raised specifically for the sport, and picking them up for their grateful owners. After which the shooters, landowner hosting the event and people used to flush out the pheasants, were treated to some hearty food and drink.

This was a wedding reception day, held in early May. Gemma had been recruited along with five other bar staff to look after the guests. The married couple were local, and the groom had been a member of the shoot for many years. This promised to be a wild day. Gemma enjoyed the bar work at the weddings, which were always entertaining. Apart from the occasional disagreements, which often happen between families on wedding days, nearly all of the guests including children would have a fun time.

The guests were due to arrive at 3pm, the staff are primed by Rory the wedding organiser, of their duties during the day and evening. Alice and Ian were the couple getting married; Alice was a local vet, and he a banker. The staff were told not to hold back on serving the drinks, but to keep them flowing. They were warned that the male guests were capable of putting away a lot of booze.

Gemma's job for the day was to look after the top table, and she had made sure that the table was laid out perfectly. Gemma noticed that there were only seven places set out. The bride, groom, both sets of parents, and the best man.

*Maybe the best man's girlfriend or wife was unable to attend? Gemma thought, or maybe his partner had preferred to sit with other relatives or friends?*

"Can I just check the placings for the top table please?" Gemma asked Rory, the wedding organiser.

Rory owned the castle and ran the shoot. He and his fiancée also ran the wedding parties, although his fiancée was away on a girly trip that weekend. He was a very dapper looking chap, with long flowing black hair. Rory was great fun. He loved the social events and knew how to organise a good party.

"There are just seven places Gemma. The best man is single, you never know your luck, he could be your type!" Rory loved flirting with the staff.

Gemma chuckled, and joined the rest of the staff for a quick bite of lunch. They all knew it would be a long afternoon and evening, with only a half hour break until some were allowed to start clocking off around 10pm.

Rory then announced "Guests are on their way, stand by your stations."

At this stage Gemma was to help greet the guests and show them to the champagne table, where the bride and groom would be standing to thank the guests for joining them in their celebrations.

It was a beautiful hot day, and the marquee was looking magnificent. The side panels were taken off to let the cool breeze through the tent. They would be replaced later when the temperatures started to drop. A bonus that the wedding organisers offered for the newlyweds was an aeroplane ride from the church, to land as a water taxi to the venue on the river below. This was a great way for the bride and groom to arrive at the reception.

Gemma knew the bride and groom, and many of the guests, but had never met the best man Graham before. Graham had been a school friend of Ian, and the two lads had spent their gap year together travelling. Graham then headed to New Zealand to take a job in sailing with the Super Challenge Yachts, whilst Ian stayed in England to become a Banker.

Graham had flown is especially for the wedding, and had been up north catching up with relatives, before arriving the day before. There was no way he was going to miss his best buddies wedding day, and was honoured to be asked to do a best man duty.

Gemma first caught sight of Graham when he stepped out of the Nissan Truck in which he had collected the newlyweds from the pontoon below. Even from a distance she could see how good looking he was.

*Oh my, he is a hottie!* Gemma thought *Let's hope there is plenty of flirting to be done.*

Rory had chosen some tight fitting tops and sexy mini-skirts for the barmaids to wear. They were classy and of French maid style. He also chose pretty ladies and gentlemen to be his bar staff. As long as they did not flirt with the bride or groom, then Rory was happy for the staff to flirt with whoever they wanted to keep the guests happy. Gemma had always had fun at these events, but so far had never met any suitable boyfriend material. She knew Graham lived in New Zealand, so she wasn't holding any hope of a relationship with him, he certainly wouldn't be soul mate material. However there could be some fun to have.

Graham held out his hand to greet Gemma and introduced himself.

*He has manners as well as good looks.* Gemma thought as she melted at his stunning deep blue eyes.

*This is going to be a flirty evening.* She thought, and imagined herself having a smoochy dance with him later, as he didn't seem to have a female in tow.

Rory invited everyone to take their seats. Gemma waited on the top table and filled the glasses of the bride and groom first. She snuck a glance at Graham, who was gazing at her from the other end of the table. He smiled and winked at her whilst she filled his glass with a cool crisp measure of Sancerre.

Gemma found the bride's father very cheeky. He too kept winking at her and even pinched her bottom as she was filling his glass. She pulled away, and noticed Graham giggling at what he saw. The bride's father Eric, was a good looking chap for his age. He was well into his fifties, still with a full head of hair, which was slightly greying. The bride's mother Christine was rather large and a bit sour looking, probably because she had to put up with Eric's provocative banter to the barmaids.

The food was served, and by the time the desserts came out, the party was in full flow. Graham was fiddling with a piece of paper which had his speech on it.

"Are you getting nervous?" Gemma asked

"Yes, it is the first speech that I have ever made." replied Graham

"You will be fine." Gemma laughed encouragingly

Graham then wrote on the back of one of the pieces of paper.

Meet me outside after the speeches!!!!

Gemma smiled, and carried on filling the glasses ready for the champagne toast.

She had clocked that all the bridesmaids were under ten. Often at weddings the bridesmaids or the maids of honour attract the attention of the best man, but at this wedding there were no eligible suitors. This left the best man up for grabs.

The speeches went well. Graham's speech delighting the guests with the naughties that the lads got up to in their younger years.

The wedding cake cutting was next on the agenda, with more champagne flutes to be filled. Graham kept on winking at Gemma as he got up to go outside. At the time she thought this inappropriate and didn't follow. She thought it would be good for him to wait.

The evening guests started to arrive at about 7pm. The band set up their equipment. A seven piece rhythm and blues band with two saxophone players. One of the best bands in the area.

Graham walked passed Gemma and asked "What time are you off?"

"Around 10pm." came Gemma's reply

"Great, I can find out more about you then, I think you are stunning and want to get to know you more."

The staff were allowed to start to clock off at around ten, when it left only four members behind the bar. Those that wanted to earn more on the late shift.

The band had managed to get most of the guests up dancing with their choice of music. Such a good band. Graham had been fooling about on the dance floor, but didn't make too much of a fool of himself. Gemma noticed that he had a real good style and couldn't help but be turned on by him. Soon after ten, Gemma had clocked off. Alice the bride was well trolleyed by that time and dragged Gemma onto the dance floor.

"Thank you so much Gemma, you and the rest of the team have put on a really good effort of looking after us."

Gemma had met Alice a few times in the pub, but didn't know her that well.

Within minutes of Gemma arriving on the dance floor, Graham appeared and started to dance provocatively beside her. She enjoyed the attention and responded, giving him the attention he had been suggesting all evening. They danced to a couple more tracks, before Graham led Gemma outside. He took her around to the side of the marquee, having grabbed a bottle of champers on the way and a couple of glasses; he poured her a drink whilst they sat on the bench overlooking the lake. It was a clear night and there seemed to be millions of stars in the sky. The champagne soon went to Gemma's head.

"Gemma we can enjoy here and now, but I can't give you anymore."

Graham was kissing Gemma's neck. She was enjoying it. But pulled away.

"I don't do one night stands, I don't sleep around."

Gemma was trying to keep control of her emotions. But Graham smelt good. He was wearing aftershave that turned her on, a good make too, that did what it said on the bottle and lasted for hours. With the smell of aftershave/pheromones and the taste of the champers, Gemma let Graham lead her away.

"It's quiet now, let's sneak in the loos." Graham suggested as he held her hand.

The wedding event hired the Exmoor luxury loos, which were very popular with many events and very luxury. Even after a days use, they seemed very fresh, and very private.
He led her into the ladies side of the mobile and closed the door behind them.

"Shush, someone's coming." Whispered Gemma

The couple stood silent for a minute, trying not to giggle, whilst a guest had a quick piddle in one of the loos.

Then as soon as the guest had gone, Gemma responded to Grahams persistent caressing and kissing. Before she knew it, she had one foot on the toilet, and with her back up against the wall she allowed him to reach up inside her. He thrusted again and again, slow and passionate, until he could hold himself no more and with a few more urgent thrust, emptied himself in her. Gemma responded when feeling him grow inside her, she moved with him until she too could hold back no more.

# Should It Happen To A Barmaid?

## *Four*

The Dolphin Inn is situated in a small coastal village known as Kingston, near Kingsbridge in South Devon. A popular pub for the local community of about 300 plus coastal hikers and walkers who use the pub as a B&B stop over, also a great place to have lunch or supper.

Gerry the Landlord was looking for extra bar staff for the summer, and had been surprised about the overwhelming response that he had to the advert he put in the local gazette. Gerry managed to narrow his selection down to three applicants, but then couldn't make his mind up. He then came up with the idea of having all of the three short listed girls on a one night trial each.

"Right lads." Gerry announced in the local end of the bar. "You are going to have to help me on the selection of this year's summer barmaid."

The lads chuckled; various comments were thrown back at Gerry.

"Well I hope you have selected some hot totty for us to choose from?" shouted Lee

"How many applicants applied?" came the comment from Lance

"We can't wait, when is the first one in for trial?" Viv asked

"Calm down boys, this is serious stuff, you will have to

put up with her for most of the summer, so behave and be nice!"

Gerry was then worried that the lads would be too fired up, and put the young ladies off working for him. A barmaid front of house can be a good business investment, if she is efficient at her job, and pretty with it too.

The girls were unaware of Gerry's idea of a short list voting system. This in a way was probably a good thing. All they knew is that they were on a day's trial so would try hard to deliver what was expected of them.

First up was Samantha, tall, dark haired, with a fit figure. Samantha had qualified as a solicitor, but then took maternity leave after having her first child. She wanted to stay off full time work for another six months, so a job in the local seemed inviting. Her hubby Steve could babysit for a few hours in the evenings, giving Samantha a way to socialise and a change from her days which were filled with baby minding.

Gerry thought Samantha deserved a short list place due to her elegant looks, her knowledge of the local area which is good for the walkers and hikers, and her light hearted banter which she had with the locals.

The lads were taken with Samantha, she worked efficiently behind the bar. Being in here thirties, she was able to communicate well with the walkers and hikers, by giving them direction on good walks and the next great place for them to eat or stay. She was also with looking after the lads by keeping them topped up with their pints of beer or larger, and wasn't offended by their cheeky banter.

Samantha was thanked by Gerry at the end of her shift.

She had got the thumbs up from the lads, and Gerry paid her at the end of her shift and said:

"I will be in touch, we have a couple of other lasses coming for a trial so will let you know by the end of the weekend."

"She was a bit of alright!" came the comment from Steve one of the lads who had stayed until late.

"We still have two others to trial as yet, so come back in tomorrow and Saturday, then make a vote." Was Gerry's reply

Next up was Mandy, a student on her summer holidays. Mandy was a first year nurse student at Bristol. She needed to earn some extra funds throughout the summer, as her student loan barely paid enough for her to live day to day on. If she wanted to enjoy the summer, then she needed to earn some extra cash to fund it.

Mandy had never worked in a bar before, she had no idea what to wear, but chose a pair of tight fitting slim jeans, a short cropped T-shirt and a huge smile. No sooner had she walked behind the bar, before the lads were leaning in drooling over their beer.

"What a little stunner!" was the comment from Bruce

"They just get prettier." Steve added

In fact Mandy was so popular with the local lads that they were all offering her a drink when she had poured their round. They also all stayed later than normal, drinking more and Gerry could hear the till roll adding up. She was also good fun with the walkers too, and although had limited local knowledge, she still managed to chat to them in her bubbly vivacious way.

It was Friday night, the darts players had arrived too. Mandy had no trouble in keeping the pints filled, the tables cleared and chat away to the customers. Every time she was offered a drink, she accepted. Thinking it would be rude not to, good for business, and had not understood the art of keeping a tab running on 'her drinks in to have later list.' So drank along with everyone else.

"Where's Mandy gone?" asked Gerry, who had his back to the bar whilst watching the darts.

"Probably done a runner." Came a random comment

Then looking over the bar Gerry shouted "Oh no she has passed out!"

He ran behind the bar to see if she was alright. Mandy was laid along the bar floor, at first Gerry thought she had fainted with the stuffy heat. He had been unaware that she had been slowly getting sozzled all night. She had been such a popular girl, that everyone offered her a drink, and being a skint student, she drank most of them.

After checking that she was still alive, they popped a cushion under her head and placed Mandy in the recovery position. Other than having to keep stepping over her to pour the pints, they left her to it. The amount of laughter that was going on, it was surprising that she slept through it. Gerry phoned her home, and her brother Tony turned up to carry her home.

"She gets my vote!" shouted Steve, what fun she has been.

Gerry added "You will have to wait lads, there is another one coming tomorrow, she maybe even more fun!"

Erica was the third short listed applicant to be given a trial night at the pub. She was a red head with a short cropped hairstyle. Quite small with a fairly round figure. Her bubbly confident character had drawn Gerry to short list her. He thought she would be able to look after herself and handle the bar too. Erica had previously worked in an Estate Agent and should have come with good customer skills.

Saturday nights are usually steady in the pub, with many eaters and fewer drinkers than on a Friday night. However the lads had decided to come in to check out the new bar talent. Gerry had promised them some voting rights, and they were keen to use them.

It was apparent from the start that Erica was not up to the job. She had started with some good banter with the locals, but then they were soon getting impatient waiting for their pints. The walkers and hikers were getting most of her attention, and unfortunately she tended to ignore the locals after a while. Gerry had to step in and help serve the locals, he didn't want to loose any customers, and wanted to keep the lads interested in the game.

At this stage, the three interviewees were unaware that they were being judged by the locals. Samantha had put up a good effort, and was sure to gather some votes. Mandy had ended up totally sozzled and they expected her to be too embarrassed to set foot in the pub again. Then there was Erica, a lovely girl, but was overwhelmed on a relatively quiet evening.

"Right lads, a private ballot will happen tomorrow

lunchtime." Gerry announced

Sunday lunchtimes were a popular session in the bar, and a good time to have the voting. The lads were chuckling among themselves. Erica had gone home, having been paid for her time and thanked by Gerry. It was about 10.30pm, the door opened and Mandy walked in.

"I am so sorry Gerry, I let you down last night. People kept buying me drinks, so I thought it would be rude not to drink them at the time." Mandy was still a little hungover, but was keen to make her apologies.

"You were a great laugh." Steve one of the lads piped up. "You get my vote!"

Gerry glared at Steve.

"What vote?" asked Mandy

Gerry realised that he had to be honest added "I have asked the local lads to help me on the decision on who to employ for the summer behind the bar, just to help me out, as I couldn't decide."

"Oh well they will think I am a lightweight Mandy giggled."

"Not at all, you were great fun until you disappeared on the floor; we were worried for a while, but then had us all in stitches." Gerry laughed and added I will let you know tomorrow afternoon.

Mandy left the bar thinking that she had blown her chances, she desperately needed to earn some cash, she thought that it was a shame she let herself down.

It was Sunday lunchtime and Gerry rang the bell on the bar.

"Right chaps, we have counted the voting, and in third place is Erica."

"Good, she kept me waiting for my beer I nearly walked out." Was the comment from Bruce

"Second place goes to." Gerry paused teasing the chaps "Second place goes to Samantha."

There was a cheer.

"But lads you must promise not to make Mandy drink her drinks bought for her whilst she is on duty behind the bar."

Gerry added "Voting over I will ring Mandy and give her the news, I am sure she will be well chuffed."

# Should It Happen To A Barmaid?

## *Five*

Mandy had settled well into pub life, now knowing her limitations when accepting drinks from customers. Gerry was pleased with the choice which he and the local lads had made. Mandy was popular with all, and a breath of fresh air for the pub. Although at times, she tended to attract too much attention. This was a worry for Gerry the landlord. Mandy tried to dress down, and wear some frumpy but tidy clothes, but she had already made an imprint into the local lad's brains.

They were not going to let her forget passing out on her interview night in a hurry, but she enjoyed the banter and attention.

It was the day of the local cricket match, and Kingston team were due to play Modbury in the local league. A marquee had been set up as a bar and shaded seating area beside the cricket pitch in the meadow close to the pub. These matches were always popular in the village and were well supported by the locals wanting to cheer on their team.

Mandy had been recruited by Gerry for the day to work behind the bar in the Marquee during the day, and her usual shift in the pub in the evening. She was pleased to be offered extra hours. Gerry knew that the local lads would support the bar with Mandy behind it, and he should sell lots of beer, along with soft refreshments.

It was a scorching hot day in June; Mandy helped Gerry

set up the bar early in the morning. Her chosen outfit for the day shift was her skinny fit red cord jeans and cropped tight T-shirt.

"Don't you want to cover yourself up a bit?" Gerry asked "The lads will be drooling over you again!"

"But It is so hot." replied Mandy "Too hot for jeans, but I thought shorts would be even more revealing."

"Have you got a skirt to wear?" quizzed Gerry

"Only mini-skirts, nothing longer"

"Oh well stick with the jeans, hopefully you will be safer." was Gerry's reply

There was a good crowd of supporters for the match. The Modbury team was first to bat, and scored 96 all out. There followed a short break for lunch, where team members were treated to a hog roast, which had been provided by local farmer James Tucker with his mobile unit. James took along his helper Les to help carve the deliciously tasty meat from the cooked carcase.

"Another pint please my dear." Les asked Mandy "This is thirsty work."

"No problem Les. Gerry told me to keep you topped up, so have as many as you like." Mandy handed Les his pint of larger.

The Kingston boys were queuing up for their beers, and Mandy had a rush of work for a while. Gerry stepped in to lend a hand, which was just as well as the team were restricted to one pint each at lunchtime until after their game had finished.

"Come on lads, go steady." shouted Gerry "We don't want any accidents."

After lunch it was the Kingston's team turn to bat, and they stormed into a fast rhythm, scoring 56 runs from the first three wickets.

Craig was next up. He was a very good looking lad, and Mandy had noticed him when the lads had queued up for their beers. Craig was very fit and Mandy couldn't help staring at his muscular arms. They had made brief eye contact, and Craig had smiled at Mandy whilst she was serving another customer. Unfortunately she was unable to get to serve Craig's beer as the wally she was serving couldn't make up his mind what he wanted to drink. Gerry had poured Craig's beer and Craig had left the marquee without Mandy getting to even say hello.

Mandy then was craning her neck to see how Craig was getting on batting.

*Mmmmmmmmme she thought,* as he made some good fast runs.

Duncan the lad bowling suddenly lost concentration. He threw the ball directly at Craig's body, hitting him in the ribs. Craig crumpled to the ground. Fortunately, Phil the Doctor was one of the spectators, and he attended to Craig.

"He will be OK. Nothing broken, he will just have a few sore ribs." Phil announced

"I am so sorry." came the reaction from Duncan "I am not trying to kill off the opposition."

Everyone laughed, although it hurt Craig to laugh and he coughed.

"We will sit Craig in the marquee for a while, where Mandy can keep an eye on him, she is training to be a nurse after all." Announced Phil

Mandy was delighted to look after Craig.

*Great,* she thought. *I will have the chance to chat to him with only a few people about.*

"I am happy to sit in the marquee for a while with Mandy." beamed Craig

"You are probably saying that it hurts more than it does, just to get her attention!" piped up Gerry

Mandy was very nervous, as she found Craig so attractive, she was trembling and full of butterflies. She believed in fate, and he was the fittest chap there that day, this was a great opportunity to make a quick impression on him.

The match was still playing, and although Craig was interested in Mandy, he was also keen to watch the game. He had helped the team with a few extra runs before he was injured, and it looked as if his team were going to win. Duncan had been taken off as bowler after his miss, and had taken a seat with the reserves, holding his head low and his tail between his legs.

Mandy didn't want to interrupt Craig's enthusiasm for the game, but at the same time longed for his attention. Craig by this time was feeling much better, and the cricket match reaching its climax, he left the chair and went outside to support his team

"We must catch up later." Craig smiled and winked at Mandy as he left the marquee.

*What does that mean?* Mandy thought. She didn't want to be too hopeful, but at the same time although she had men falling at her feet, she had trouble in letting her guard down, and had become fussy with whom she spent her time with.

Mandy pushed the thought aside, and served another customer at the bar.

"Watch that one Mandy. He is a bit of a heartbreaker. If you want just a bit of fun, then enjoy." Mark had given her some wise words.

"I can handle it." Mandy replied " I am still looking for Mr Right, and I am sure I will be looking for a few more years yet!"

The match was soon over, and everyone piled back into the bar. Mandy was too busy to dwell on the thought of anything happening with Craig, although she did however enjoy a cheeky glance or two.

Kingston the home team had won the match, and they were going to celebrate well into the evening. Gerry closed the bar on the field at six, and the Modbury team headed home which was a few miles away, whilst the victorious winning Kingston team headed to the pub where the celebrations got in full swing.

Craig was pacing himself, still suffering from sore ribs, he didn't want to risk getting totally drunk and falling over. He was paying Mandy a lot of attention, with the other lads in the bar, he wanted to have her full attention to himself, and she responded with flirting with him too, in between serving drinks to the others.

The lads were fed on the leftovers from the hog roast, and many started to head off home, or were supported home by their wives or girlfriends.

It was 9.30pm and Craig offered to walk Mandy home.

"That would be nice, thank you; I am off in about ten minutes."

Mandy had taken on board what Mark had said about Craig, but at the same time she didn't want to miss the opportunity to have some time alone with him. Although he may be a heart breaker, she knew he was well known in the area, so she hoped she could trust him.

She had accepted a couple of glasses of wine towards the end of the evening, having learned her lesson before; she restricted herself to only two glasses whilst she was working.

As they left the pub Gerry shouted "Straight home mind, be a gentleman Craig!"

"I always am!" He replied.

They were barely out of the door when the two embraced, they couldn't keep their hands off each other.

"Careful ouch!" Craig spoke softly, his ribs were still hurting.

The electricity running between the pair was turning them both on. Craig grabbed hold of Mandy's hand.

"Let's go to the tent."

The couple giggled and made their way to the marquee tent in the field, which had been the bar for the day where they had first set eyes on each other.

Craig sat in the seat and put an arm out invitingly to Mandy.

"Now nurse Mandy, you can give me whatever treatment you feel fit."

Mandy couldn't resist him. She kissed him slowly and passionately. Craig ran his hands over her body, slipping his hand under her T shirt, undoing her bra, exploring her breasts and nipples. She responded by running her tongue down his neck slowly, then back up to his ear and whispered "More."

He unzipped her jeans and she unzipped his. Craig moaned approvingly.

"Can you take me?" he asked and added "All of me?"

"Yes." She replied and guided him into her.

Mandy was ready to accept all of him. They tried to keep as quiet as possible but both groaned with pleasure as they reached heaven together.

# Should It Happen To A Barmaid?

## *Six*

The summer had flown by. It was soon Mandy's last shift working at the pub before heading back to University.

"Would you consider coming back to work for me again?" asked Gerry

He was disappointed to be loosing Mandy, she was a popular barmaid. He was sure that she had helped boost the takings over the summer.

"Yes of course, I would love to come back." she replied

She had lots of fun whilst working at the pub, had managed to save some money and had met lots of interesting people. She enjoyed a touch of romance too, but nothing lasting.

Mandy was doing her usual checks for stock levels of drinks in the chiller when a lady walked in through the door and came up to the bar. Recognising her, Mandy said

"Hi Marion, what can I get you to drink?"

"Nothing, I have a proposition for you." Replied Marion

"That sounds interesting, what did you have in mind?"

"Well, you know my husband Simon who drinks in here? I am not sure how I can put this, but are you in need of some extra cash?" Marion asked

"It is my last shift here before heading back to Uni next week, I could do with some extra cash." Mandy was unsure of what Marion was going to ask her to do.

"How about I offer you £100 if you would be a Honey Trap for Simon?"

Mandy blushed and laughed. *What is a Honey Trap she thought?* Having never heard of it. She had fancied Simon, there was no denying that. He was a fit looking chap, her typical stereotype, and in his mid-thirties. She had flirted with him once or twice over the bar, but knowing that he was well married, and Marion his wife was known to be a bit of a dragon, Mandy had just left it as friendly banter with him.

Marion went on to say "I am afraid I just don't trust him anymore, he has become a bit distant and sulky. I fear he is either having an affair already or looking for one."

Mandy felt sorry for Marion. She had never really got to know her, and always thought that she was a bit fierce. Maybe it was Marion's way of not trusting Simon, or the women around him?

"I will double it, how about £200, but you will need to give me proof."

"What exactly is a Honey Trap?" Mandy asked

"You will need to be a temptress, to see if Simon will play away. I would like to think that he is devoted to me, but I have been going out of my mind thinking that we are living a lie."

"So I don't have to sleep with him?"

"No. Just see if you can get him to meet you on the beach maybe? Text me when you are on your way down there and I will come down looking for you both. Well him anyway."

200£ was a lot of money to Mandy. She did fancy Simon, but could she lead him on? She also loved a challenge.

Marion added "Simon was planning on coming out for a drink tonight after work, about eightish. He had a client to see early evening. He said not to make him supper as he was going to have a pint before coming home. I think either he is having an affair already, or just doesn't want to come home."

The couple had an accounting company, which they ran from home. Client evening visits were often made. Simon was more of a pub drinker than Marion, and recently he had started to come in more frequently, so maybe Marion's hunch was true.

"Ok I will do it." Mandy smiled at Marion, not only did she feel sorry for her, but she also fancied Simon, so thought she had nothing to lose.

"On one condition though. I want to tell somebody else about the plan, just in case I am accused of doing anything outrageous. I would like to come back and work here in the future."

"That's fine, you can tell Gerry if you like?"

"No, I am not sure he would approve! I will tell the chef Luke." Mandy went into the kitchen where Luke was prepping the food for evening meals.

"Are you sure you can handle it?" asked Luke

"You know me, I am always up for a challenge, and

besides, I could do with the money."

Mandy encouraged Luke to come out of the kitchen to have a quick word with Marion. It was the only way Mandy was sure that Marion was serious about the offer, and would keep her word about the money.

"It has to be tonight." Explained Marion "If you text me when you are on your way down to the beach, then I can follow you down there shortly after."

Mandy shrugged her shoulders.

"OK, it's worth a go. I am not sure I am that fast at pulling, but I will see what I can do."

"Even if you find out what his problem is, if he is unhappy? Then it is worth paying you for."

Marion left the pub as the early evening drinkers started to pile in. Gerry appeared from the office.

"What was Marion doing in here earlier?"

"Oh just after some info on B&B for a friend who is coming down for an Autumn wedding." Mandy replied

Mandy enjoyed having a flirt, and to have the wife's consent on this occasion, to chat up one of the best looking chaps in the village was a bonus. And to be paid for it too.

The bar was busy that night. Many of the local lads had turned up knowing that it was Mandy's last shift. Most of them offered her drinks, it was a shame that she was driving later, that's if she did the job properly, and pulled Mr Fitty!

When Simon walked into the bar, her heart missed a beat. She became a little flustered and blushed. Simon was wearing a crisp white shirt. He always dressed smartly; even in casual wear he looked hot. He had also enjoyed the good weather, and had a lovely glowing tan. It was about 8.30pm and Mandy had promised to text Marlon when Simon had walked into the pub.

"What can I get you to drink?"

Mandy held her gaze at Simon, looking straight into his eyes, and followed up with a friendly smile.

"Pint of Cider please Mandy."

"Have you had a good day?" she asked

"Yes thank you, I have been looking forward to a pint for a couple of hours." He carried on

"Is this your last shift?"

"Yes, I have to return to University at the end of the week."

"That's a shame; I haven't got to know you properly."

"I will be back in the Autumn for a week if they will have me again." Mandy held her gaze at Simon.

One of the other lads piped up. "We will have to put up with grumpy Gerry again!"

The lads all laughed.


Simon then chatted to various chaps around the bar,

but would frequently glance across at Mandy, and she responded with a smile.

*Maybe he is a player? Can I go through with this? I quite like him, shame I didn't get to know him earlier in the summer. If only I had known his marriage was on the rocks.* Mandy thought.

As the evening wore on Simon joined in the banter as the lads were teasing Mandy. She was receiving plenty of attention from all of them.

Simon asked Mandy for another pint. It was his third, and he was relaxing nicely.

"Haven't you a home to go to?" teased Mandy

"I am not in a hurry to go back there, I am having far too much fun here. Would you like a drink?"

Mandy wanted to accept Simon's offer, but she had already had one drink and if she was going to go through with Marion's trapping request she needed to stay sober and within the legal drinking limits.

Simon lived within the village, a short walking distance from the pub. He was often known to leave his car in the car park and collect it in the morning.

"What time do you finish?" Simon asked Mandy

"Gerry is taking over the bar duties at about 10pm, I was planning on having a couple of drinks then."

Mandy couldn't help thinking about Marion, and was wondering what Simon was going to offer.

"How about we take a bottle of bubbly down to the beach? Do you have a car here?"

The bar had thinned out. Simon was giving Mandy much more attention, and she was able to respond in a flirty way whilst the bar was quieter. With that her phone bleeped. She knew it would be Marion asking how she was getting on.

The message read. IS HE STILL IN THE PUB?

Mandy looked at Simon. Where would she lay her loyalties? Knowing the local beach is about a mile past Simon's house. If she went to the beach with him, then they would have to pass his house. Did she want Marion to spoil what could be some fun? Mandy often attracted married men. Her bubbly vivacious nature, good figure and pretty face, often had the men falling at her feet.

Mandy replied to the text. YES

Marion replied TEXT ME WHEN HEADING TO BEACH IF YOU GO.

Mandy responded with OK

Mandy smiled at Simon, the time was 9.30pm. She turned and headed into the kitchen to find Luke. She wanted to scream loudly.

"How's it going Mandy, have you pulled yet?"

She whispered to Luke "I've pulled, but I like him and would rather get to know Simon than do a favour for Marion."

"Think of the money!" was Luke's reply

"Sometimes money isn't everything." And she walked back into the bar.

As she arrived at the bar she heard Gerry saying "Nice bottle of bubbly to take home to the wife tonight Simon?" whilst handing Simon his change.

Mandy blushed thinking *So Simon thinks I am going to the beach with him?*

Simon rolled his eyes towards the door, tempting her as she walked into the bar. He still had a couple of slurps left in his glass.

"You can head off now if you like Mandy, come back in for a drink tomorrow before you head back to Bristol." Gerry was going to miss Mandy's presence and was keen to encourage her back.

Mandy, for a split second was unsure whether or not to follow Simon, or would she text Marion to say they were off to the beach? She had to make a split decision. Collecting her bag and coat, she opened up her phone and texted Marion.

I HAVE GONE HOME. SIMON IS STILL IN THE PUB. I WILL MEET YOU TOMORROW TO TELL YOU WHAT I FOUND OUT.

Mandy left the pub, Simon was waiting outside for her. He put his arm warmly around her shoulders and they walked towards her car. Instead of turning left to the beach and past Simon's house, Mandy turned right towards Arymer Cove a couple of miles away. She parked in the isolated car park beside the beach. She reach for a CD, she chose Adele 19. Simon kissed Mandy, she couldn't resist him.

He opened the bottle of champers. Mandy had grabbed a couple of glasses from the bar when leaving the pub. Gerry hadn't noticed as he was serving another customer at the time.

They toasted the night. Mandy had no loyalties to Marion, and from what Marion had said, their marriage was on the rocks. Simon and Mandy talked for a while.

"Am I one of many?" she asked teasingly

"No" came Simons reply "I haven't been happy for a while at home, we argue a lot."

Simon had been married before, and was the type who would want fun and excitement in a relationship. The type who wouldn't settle for long, before seeking another pleasure.

"Let's enjoy here and now." Simon spoke softly to Mandy.

She moved over to sit on the passenger seat facing him. Slowly undoing the button on his crisp white shirt, whilst kissing him passionately. He responded, he slipped his hands under her T-shirt, undoing her bra and fondled her breasts. Mandy gently poured some champagne teasingly into his mouth, whilst holding his gaze. She leant down and licked his lips. He was turned on; she slowly undid the zip on his jeans, again holding his gaze. He responded by doing the same and she slipped out of her jeans.

The couple made love to the track Chasing Pavements from the Adele CD.

Mandy met up with Marion the following lunchtime.

"He is unhappy, but I don't think he is having an affair

yet" stated Mandy

"Thank you, here is the £200, Simon came home at about 11.30 after the pub closed. He fell asleep on the couch, I guess he was pissed."

"Just give me "£100, it will help me with petrol and some groceries for my trip back to Bristol."

"OK, here you are." Marion handed over the notes.

"Thanks and good luck with your marriage."

Mandy was hoping that she may meet up with Simon again when she returned in the Autumn, *That's if he hasn't run off with anyone else before then.*

# Should It Happen To A Barmaid?

## *Seven*

Dartmouth is a stunning town, situated on the banks of the river Dart in South Devon. Every year in the month of August, there is a pilgrimage of boats flocking up the river Dart to compete in the Royal Dartmouth Yacht sailing regatta. The event is held over four days, from Thursday through until Sunday.

The hundreds of boats, from dingies to 100ft super yachts all containing a number of crew on board. Most of the crew are fit muscular men. There are some females, and the random boat with an all-girl crew, which obviously attracts a lot of attention from the other crews.

'Yachties' as they are fondly known, are normally a picture of health, sporting a colourful tan from the hours they spend on the water. Not only does the regatta attract sailors, but also thousands of people flock to the port to watch this colourful event, with the spectacular sight of boats heading in and out of the estuary with full sails up. There is also a great buzz and atmosphere around the town. The bars are full of party goers, both during the day and night, and well into the early hours of the morning.

Julie had been recruited by the Yacht club to work behind the bar at the club house during the day, and in the club marquee in the evenings. The club marquee is exclusive to the sailors, serving breakfast for the hungry crews in the mornings, and food, drinks and entertainment throughout the evenings.

This night was promising to be particularly busy, with the main entertainment being Antiqua Joe. A Rastafarian singing entertainer, who sang really good reggae music. Julie and the other barmaids who were recruited for the evening session were really excited, at the promise of hundreds of fit chaps enjoying a night out partying after sailing; it was always a good 'craic'.

The boats headed back into port at about 4pm. The weather had been kind, with plenty of sunshine and shed loads of wind. The crews normally head into the bars, having spent many hours on the water in the boats, and finishing by packing the sails away at the end of the day. If the wind was strong, then the crew would be very tired but exhilarated by a good days sailing. The teams that had finished in the first three were normally the rowdiest. Wanting to celebrate their efforts, and keen to find out how they were doing on the overall competition.

The daily results, along with the current standings would be posted in the club house, which is where the teams headed first. Parties would come later in the marquee. The atmosphere was always buzzing, with Julie and the other barmaids looking forward to the first jubilant crews to arrive at the clubhouse. The girls had a private competition of their own, voting for the first 10/10 chap they could spot. And if they pulled him, then the other girls would all have to treat her to free drinks the following day.

On this particular day, Julie had spotted who she thought was her 10/10. David was about 6ft tall, slim build, with her normal stereotype looks of dark spikey hair and blue eyes. His eyes were looking even bluer, whilst he was sporting a fabulous tan and glowing from being windswept.

"Three pints of Doombar please." David asked Julie

Julie immediately looked at one of the other barmaids, grinning and giving her a 'thumbs up'. They all knew he was a definite 10/10. All the barmaids had to agree on the 10/10 for it to be a valid vote.

*Oh my* Julie thought, as she turned her back on him whilst putting the money in the till and getting out his change. She could see his face in the mirror behind the bar, and she caught him clocking her bottom whilst looking her up and down. She took a deep breath and turned around.

"Did you win today?" she asked

"Yes we did, we had a fabulous day and intend to celebrate well tonight."

David headed back to his fellow crew members with the three pints. Julie could see them all chuckling at what comment David had made, and they all looked her way.

*I wonder what he had said to them?* She thought

Turning to the other girls who were thumbs up "Yep Julie, we agree you have found the first 10/10 today. Let's see if you can get off with him now?"

"Might find a better one yet, maybe an 11/10, the rest of the crews are not in yet." Julie smiled

"Well I don't think you will find a better one than him tonight!" Erica squealed.

The bar was buzzing, the girls were kept busy pulling the pints and the crews were all getting merry.

"I am off now for my break, will see you in the marquee later." Mandy had an hour break before doing her shift work in the marquee, the band was due to perform at 9pm, and she had her instructions to start at 8pm.

Most of the crews would be grabbing some food in the club house before partying until the early hours. Some would stay on the boats for a nap before taking a quick shower and freshen themselves up for later. Julie nipped to the loo before heading across into Dartmouth on the water taxi. The ladies and gents toilets were situated next to each other. To her delight Graham was coming out of the gents as she was walking by.

"Are you off now?" he asked

"Only for my break." She smiled "I am on duty in the marquee later."

"Great, will catch you then, we are looking forward to listening to Antiqua Joe."

"He is a great singer, and will surely have most of the crowd dancing till midnight." Julie explained

"Will you have a chance for a dance later?"

Julie replied "Yes I hope so, as I am only working the early shift."

Julie was chuffed she had bumped into Graham. Maybe she would be in for some free drinks from the other barmaids after all for finding a 10/10. She headed into town to grab a sandwich and to do a bit of girly shopping. Julie always liked the treat of going over to town in the water taxi, it was always a good place to spot some eye candy en route.

Back in the marquee later, Julie couldn't see Graham there to start with. Not that it mattered, there was plenty enough eye candy there for her to ogle at.

"Have you seen my 10/10 yet in here?" She asked Erica

"No not yet, he has probably gone for a quick nap and shower before coming out again. They were all getting rather sozzled after you had left the bar."

The crews were easily identified by the team shirts or gillets they were wearing that had been given to them by their skippers. The clothing would have the boat name either across the back, or on the lapels. The colours of the tops are normally colour co-ordinated with the boat graphics, based on a black, blue, red or grey theme. Julie was keeping an eye out for the boat name Dark & Steamy. She been part of a sailing crew herself in regattas in previous years, on a fun boat named Major Clanger, and was able to talk the jargon, scoring brownie points with the lads for doing so.

"Ey up, they have just walked in." commented Erica

"Game on then." Julie smiled

Graham strode up to the bar grinning at Julie.

"Three Tequila slammers please." He asked

Julie laughed smiling at Graham, the boys were certainly out for a fun night. The sailors usually peaked early, then collapsed early, and were usually up and ready for sailing again the following day. Some getting very squiffy, and most knowing their limits.

"Here you go." Julie placed the shorts on the bar. The lads had fun at geeing each other up before downing the drinks.

"Three Ciders now please." Graham winked at Julie.

"What's your name?" he asked

"Julie, what's yours." she replied

"Graham"

"What do you do when you are not sailing?" asked Julie

"I am a junior Doctor." He replied

*Gosh she thought, he is lovely, and a Doctor, who could want for more?*

Julie reported back to the girls behind the bar. They were all dying to know what her chat with Graham was about.

"He is a doctor, way out of my league." Julie said disappointingly.

"You shouldn't put yourself down Julie, you are lovely and a real man magnet, just wait and see." Erica was egging Julie on.

It was Antigua Joe's time to strutt his stuff and get the party going. That is just what he did. The place was a buzz, a fabulous atmosphere. The bar was lively, and Julie, along with the other barmaids, were being chatted up by many of the sailors.

Julie decided to do a sweep of the bar and collect some glasses. She was hoping to bump into Graham, and as she walked out onto the balcony to clear the glasses there, Graham touched her on the shoulder.

"Hey, let's dance." Graham asked

"I am off in five minutes, I will come and find you then."

Julie headed back to the bar with the glasses.

" I think I've pulled." She shouted to Erica

The music was so loud.

"What? You have pulled him already?" Erica asked

"Yes, you watch." Julie gathered her bag, a glass of wine and headed over to Graham, who was leaning against the marquee post. She turned and put her thumbs up to Erica.

They danced for a while, jigging around with hundreds of happy sailors singing along to the songs.

Graham then lead Julie out of the marquee.

"Let's go to my boat."

"Is it your boat?" asked Julie

"I have shares in it, one of us has to stay on the boat as security overnight, and tonight is my turn."

Julie had no reason not to believe Graham. She followed him as he led her up the jetty.

Graham held out his hand and invited Julie aboard the yacht. It was a beautiful Sigma 362 a one design racing yacht. The couple sat on the foredeck. Taking in the delightful lights of the town, the stars and the heady atmosphere they had created.

"Come on, I will give you a guided tour."

Graham led Julie down the stairs into the cabin of the boat. It had all the luxuries that a yacht should have. Plush galley kitchen, shower, toilet and three bunk cabins. Graham grabbed a bottle of fizz out of the fridge along with a couple of glasses, and led Julie into the fore cabin. He paused to put on a cd on the music system. He turned to Julie and kissed her.

U2 was his cd of choice. Julie loved the music and responded to Graham's attention.

"Are you ok?" he asked

"Yes thank you, I am having a good time." Julie sipped more of her fizz.

 Knowing that Graham had drunk quite a lot. But he still managed to put her at ease with his gentle attention.

Her favourite U2 track came on : All that you can't leave behind. She melted in his arms.  He slowly undressed her and she lay back down on the mattress in the cabin. Graham started to whisper the song to her. She was at his mercy, she had no control of her emotions. She responded to his slow touch, working his way down her body. He kissed her from head to toes, she lay back and enjoyed every moment. Julie responded by gently kissing and caressing Grahams neck, working her way down his body. She ran her tongue down his thighs very slowly, teasing him as she turned back up his body. Admiring his eight pack on the way.

*He has a heavenly body, the other girls will not believe this!* Julie didn't want the evening to end.

The boat rocked gently as they reached ultimate satisfaction together.

Julie had to get off the boat early before the other crew members arrived for sailing duties. She headed back into the yacht club for a shower. As she walked through the door, Barry the manager came out of the office.

"Walk of shame is it then Julie?" he inquired

Julie was delighted with her catch.

"I ended up with Graham who's a doctor." She smiled

"They can be anything they like when they are away at regattas, don't believe him. They always say they are a doctor, they think it gives them more pulling power."

Julie's heart sank. *How stupid I am!* She thought. *Oh well I pulled a 10/10 and the other girls owe me lots of drinks now.*

# Should It Happen To A Barmaid?

## *Eight*

The rugby club is situated on the top of a hill in Kingsbridge, a quiet little estuary town in South Devon. Nicky had worked there for six weeks, she was enjoying every minute of it. Welcoming hot sweaty fit chaps to enjoy their pints of beer at the end of a hard afternoon's rugby match was a joy.

Not only did the local lads support the bar, but also the visiting teams. There seemed to be an unlimited constant flow of new talent arriving. The visiting team members were just as lovely, fit and tasty as the home team.

One of the longer serving barmaids asked Nicky if she would like to go to the Ladies Evening event at the rugby club in Exeter.

"It is great fun, would you like to come along Nicky?" asked Helen. "We normally catch a mini bus up there, and taxi back at various times." She added

"Sounds like fun, I have only been to Ladies nights at the races, this sounds a nice change." Nicky had agreed to go along out of curiosity.

"What shall I wear?" Nicky asked

"Well, we will be dancing till midnight, so something like a party dress would go down well. It is great fun, you will enjoy the entertainment."

The girls arrived at the Rugby club in Exeter. Nicky was

impressed with the view of the smart pitch below, with large stands beside the pitch. They were greeted to a champagne reception on arrival. The tables were circular tables laid out with eight places on each. A three course dinner was on the menu.

"You will like what else is on the menu." laughed Helen.

Nicky noticed once seated, that there was one empty place on each table.

"That's strange, there seems to be one empty space on every single table. What's that all about?" she inquired to Helen.

"That's for the entertainment, you wait and see, I guarantee, you will be pleasantly surprised!" Helen smiled.

Once the ladies were all seated, Gordon picked up the microphone.

"Welcome ladies, I hope you are ready for this evening's entertainment, I hope you have an enjoyable evening. Let me introduce your first guest."

The DJ put on the first music track Rubox by Robbie Williams. The ladies started clapping in tune to the song.

"May I introduce to you Will!" Gordon announced.

Will came dancing through the door to the sound of the track. He stopped for a second, slipped off his jacket, which he the chucked over his shoulder, then seductively danced to his allocated table. The ladies were cheering, clapping and dancing their top bodies whilst sat. All wondering which table Will had been allocated.

*Mmmmm I wonder which table he is heading for?*
Thought Nicky, having figured out why a space had been
left on each table.

Will worked his way around his allocated table and kissed
all the ladies on the cheek, probably checking them out as
he did  Then he sat down.

The DJ let the Robbie Williams theme tune CD run on.
The next track was Viva Life on Mars. The ladies started
clapping to the beat.

"Ladies let me introduce Tony!" Gordon announced and
the ladies cheered.

Tony appeared through the door wearing a cowboy
hat, he was wearing a waistcoat over his checked shirt.
He also had on a cowboy pair of chaps. With his jet
black hair, and designer stubble, he was a vision of pure
masculinity. He slowly and seductively undid the buttons
on his shirt down to his waist, revealing his slightly hairy
chest covering what looked like a decent six pack of
muscle. He too danced his way to his allocated table, to
the thrill of the ladies being kissed before he sat down to
join them.

*Oh my who are we going to get on our table, they just
seem to be getting better and better!* Nicky thought.

Gordon announced the next player. "Next up is Warren!"

The DJ had changed the music, and Warren entered to the
sound of Rod Stewart singing Do You Think I'm Sexy?
And Warren definitely was that.

Warren was most of the ladies ultimate vision of 'sex on

legs'. Tall blonde, smouldering blue eyes and shoulders as wide as a house.

Warren, to the delight of the ladies, stood there showing off his physique. He slipped off his jacket, he undid his shirt, removing it, and just leaving a bow tie. Warren had an eight pack chest and abdominal muscles. He was also well tanned. The ladies cheered and clapped and many were beckoning him to their tables.

*Oh my, whoever is coming through that door next, and what part of their clothing will they be removing?* Nicky was shy and reserved, and although had enjoyed flirting whilst working behind the bar in their own rugby club, she had never witnessed anything like this before. She was beginning to wonder if she should have come along after all.

Gordon then introduced Jake.

"Now then ladies, are you ready for the prettiest player on the team? Jake will you walk through that door please?"

The whole room almost exploded. The ladies could hardly contain themselves. They cheered, clapped and wolf whistled. Jake stopped at the door. He was another tall dark superman vision, dark with baby blue eyes and very long eyelashes. He was a young rugby player, and was less rugged than the others.

The DJ had selected Cold Play "Magic." And as far as Nicky was concerned he was the best in her eyes. Jake slowly removed his jacket, he ripped open his shirt. The girls loved it and cheered him on. He too had an eight pack of muscles and was bare chested. Nicky's eyes were drawn to his muscular arms. Helen too was beside herself with admiration for this hunky figure walking towards their table. He kissed all of the ladies in turn and took his seat. Nicky was speechless. They had definitely drawn the best hottie!

There were only eight tables in the room, filled with seven ladies on each, and eight of the fittest, best looking rugby players in the team, who were all single and up for a laugh. Gordon introduced the rest of the players to join the tables. All took off items of clothing including Luke, who stripped down to his fetching boxer shorts, revealing his very fit thighs.

The lads were primed to be wine waiters for their tables for the evening, they kept the ladies glasses topped up and ensured they shared their attentions with all of them. Nicky was reserved at first, but once the wine had kicked in, she relaxed and started to loosen up.

Part of the theme for the evening, was to help raise funds for injured players. An auction of pledges was held which raised £2000. The ladies were bidding more as the merrier they were getting.

Gordon announced the first lot.

"Lot one is two tickets to watch the Exeter game on Saturday week."

The ladies were bidding well, being egged on by their token player on their table. The tickets made £100.

"The next lot up for auction is Luke's Autobiography book, signed by the Author. Come on ladies dig deep, it is for a good cause." Gordon was egging the ladies on too.

The book fetched £50, which was good as a normal copy unsigned would retail for £20.

"Lot three is a week in a cottage in Cornwall."

One of the lads parents had put the cottage forward. It reached a value of £550 and looked well worth the bid.

Gordon carried on as the ladies were downing more wine.

"Lot four is dinner with Luke!" a cheer went up.

"This offer includes being taken to a top restaurant in Exeter, having a three course meal, drinks and you get to spend three quality hours with Luke. The offer includes a taxi ride home." Gordon added "Who will start the bid at fifty pounds?"

"£80" shouted Helen

"£90" shouted Ruth from another table.

Gordon didn't need to gee the ladies up, they were keen. The bid went to £300 to Ruth, who was a bit of a beauty herself, so Luke was well pleased.

"Next up is lot five, a night at the cinema, seeing a film of your choice with any player here. He will take you for a curry after"

There was plenty of laughter and giggling.

"Come on ladies, what's it worth? Has to be £100?" Gordon encouraged them.

The bidding soon went up to £350. Susan was the lady determined to win the bid. She was a wealthy divorcee, and looked up for a bit of fun.

"She will be dragging him off to see Fifty Shades Of Grey, Susan is a real goer!" Helen informed Nicky.

"Ladies we now have our last lot to offer, which is a day away with the rugby team on tour. The prize includes overnight stay too, as it is one of their longer distance tournament matches."

Again the ladies didn't hold back on raising their hands at the offer. Bidding was fast and furious, with two of the ladies Jill and Sarah going bid for bid. Jill got the final bid at £750.

"Thank you ladies. That is the end of the auction. Thank you for your generosity. Enjoy the rest of your evening."

The music started again, I'm Sexy and I know It. The lads all chose one lady from the table to dance with.

*Gosh the evening just gets more interesting.* Nicky thought, as one by one the lads worked their way around the tables to dance with all the ladies. Nicky couldn't take her eyes off Luke dancing in his boxer shorts. She was a leg lady, and his muscles were bulging fabulously.

Jake was a good dancer too, with plenty of rhythm. She had fun dancing seductively with him when it was her turn.

By this time it was Helen who was having the most fun. She snuck off outside with Luke and had some fun in the stands. By this time many of the players were dancing naked on the dance floor. Nicky was so embarrassed.

It was when Helen then headed off with another player Tony, that Nicky called it a day and got a taxi home.

She had only known Helen a short while, but *Honestly, two men in one night!* That was the limit.

## Nine

Many females struggle in relatio<br>
wrong where romance is involved a<br>
It is human nature to fall in love. Ther<br>
who meet their soul mate early on in l<br>
many that don't.

As the song goes 'It only takes a minute<br>
that saying has become for millions of coup<br>
have the opportunity to meet many pe<br>
their time behind the bar. Be it the opposit<br>
they prefer, then the same sex. Instant attract<br>
always mutual. It helps if the two are attracted<br>
other, unless of course one of the couple are spo<br>
That is when things can become really complicate

Nicky was working her shift behind the bar in the E.<br>
Inn. a popular pub within the market town of Modb<br>
The pub is a drinking pub that attracts many locals a<br>
visitors throughout the year. One of the locals 'Micl<br>
walked into the bar.

"Pint of Jail Ale please." He asked Nicky

"Yes no problem." Nicky could hardly get the words out of her mouth.

Nicky was trembling, her heart had skipped a beat. She purposely didn't fill the glass too much, as she was in fear of spilling it as her hands were shaking.

s known by the other locals in the pub. y way, he laughed and joked with all of them. uldn't take her eyes off of him.

*t be local she thought?*

s polite too, He introduced himself to Nicky.

o, I'm Mick, you probably gathered I am one of the ." Mick reached out to shake Nicky's hand.

nice to meet you. I am Nicky the new barmaid." ky smiled and reached over the bar to shake Mick's d. Mick squeezed her hand and winked. Nicky was en from that moment on.

ick turned to chat tp the other lads around the bar rea. Friday nights are always popular, like many pubs, vith drinkers enjoying their first drink of the weekend. The atmosphere was a buzz. Mick spoke to one of the lads.

"Who's the cute barmaid?" he asked.

"That's Nicky, she lives in Kingsbridge." One of the lads said.

"Mmmmm, nice figure." Mick laughed whilst looking directly at Nicky pulling a pint for another customer over the other side of the bar.

"Yes we know." Piped up Tom "She is good fun too." He added

The local band was due to play that evening in the pub, and the group had turned up with their equipment. Nicky knew that she would be busy from early doors

until at least 10.30 – 11ish.

"Who's the chap with the spikey blonde hair?" she asked Ted the landlord.

"Oh that's Mick, he is single if you are interested? Lives in the town as a local builder, a self-employed one before you ask." Ted smiled at Nicky.

Nicky was even more interested knowing that Mick is single. *Can't be as simple as that!* Nicky thought. *Maybe a rebound? I don't fancy being yet another stepping stone?* Nicky thought, as she herself had recently been dumped by her then boyfriend. She was still feeling a bit raw from the breakup, and thought that by being a barmaid, it could provide a good distraction.

Mick headed to the bar for another pint of Jail Ale.

"What do you do for a normal day job then Nicky?" he asked

"I am a receptionist in a dental practice."

"You can check out my teeth anytime." Mick revealed his huge beautiful white gleaming toothed smile. He then kept heading back to the bar topping up on Jail Ale for an excuse to chat up Nicky.

The party was in full flow. With all enjoying the great music, by local band The Penguins, the dance floor was full. Nicky noticed that even though Mick was slowly getting drunk, he had a great style of dancing, and he knew it. He often looked over to the bar, and caught Nicky watching him. He would give her a lovely smile and wink.

"Last orders please!" Ted the landlord shouted to all customers, and rang a ding dong on the bell.

Mick came up to the bar, where he found Nicky washing some glasses.

"When are you working again?" he asked

"I will be in on Tuesday night."

"Cool, I will pop in for a beer then" Mick winked at Nicky and left the pub with a few mates. He lived a close distance from the pub, and would often go back to his place with a few mates for a good chin wag and a few more beers.

Nicky was looking forward to meeting Mick again, and couldn't wait for Tuesday to arrive. She was in high spirits at work, and Rachel the receptionist commented

"Look at you Nicky, you have a spring in your step, and can't stop singing to yourself! Who have you fallen for? Come on spill the beans!" Rachel knew Nicky was well fussy with whom she fell for. Some would say she was rigid, but knowing her as Rachel did, she was really just a shy sensitive soul, and very particular as to who she gave her heart too.

"Oh it is just a chap called Mick who I met in Modbury whilst working in the Ex on Friday night.

"Don't get your heart broken Nicky, I hope you have found someone who can be your soul mate?"

Nicky smiled and replied

"He seems lovely, and makes me laugh. I can't wait to see

him again on Tuesday."

Tuesday soon came around, and Nicky rushed home from the Dental practice, having collected her dog Freddie from the doggy day care sitter on her way home. She then managed to enjoy a ten minute soak in the bath, before heading out to do her shift at the pub. The next issue she had was deciding on what to wear. Running out of time, she settled for a tight low cut T-shirt and a tight pair of slim fit jeans. The pub had a fairly relaxed atmosphere, there was no uniform to wear.

Mick was already downing a pint of Jail Ale by the time Nicky arrived. He turned to smile at her, clocking what she was wearing. Nicky blushed.

"I am off to the Journey's End in Ringmore now for a pint. I Will be back in an hour or so." Ted the landlord liked to have a tour of the local pubs, he enjoyed catching up with his fellow landlords once a week if he could.

"Ok." Nicky replied. She was well capable of looking after the bar for an hour or two, and knew that Ted would have checked all the barrels before heading off.

*Ideal, I can get some quiet time with Mick if there are not too many people in the bar.* Nicky thought.

She enjoyed being in control of the music CD system, and could choose a CD of her choice. She chose a CD by Paloma Faith.

"Nice choice of music." Mick commented

It was a good topic of conversation. They found that they had a similar choice of music.

"I personally like Snow Patrol, Coldplay and Hootie and the Blowfish." Nicky responded with

"I am into James Bay, Ed Sheeran, Jack Savoretti and the new Hosier Album is awesome."

Mick only stayed for a few pints, to Nicky's disappointment. But as he was leaving he came out with:

"I am having a party on Saturday night. You are welcome to come along."

"Thanks that would be nice, I am here until ten-ish."

"Great see you then if not before. It doesn't start until eight, so you shouldn't miss much."

Both held their gaze as Mick left the pub. Nicky was thrilled to be asked to Mick's party. The next day she booked her dog Freddie into the overnight Dog Lodge. Sometimes she felt guilty having a life and going out. But then as long as Freddie was comfortable in his overnight stay, she would be able to relax and enjoy the party without feeling she would need to rush home. She felt a good connection between her and Mick, the attraction seemed mutual. Plenty of chemistry was going on between the two of them, and she wanted to enjoy it.

Saturday night soon arrived, and again Nicky couldn't decide what to wear. Maybe her lack of confidence had made her feel less attractive. She so wanted to catch Mick's eye.

"Where are you off to tonight then? Party to go to by any chance? Ted asked Nicky, he had already heard about Mick's party.

"I have been invited to Mick's tonight; he is having a party at his place."

"Yes I had heard, and you look lovely, he can't help but notice you." Ted smiled encouragingly at Nicky

He added "I thought there was a spark between you too, but be careful, don't fall too quickly. Mick has just come out of a long and tricky relationship, take it steady."

"Don't worry I will uncle Ted." Nicky replied teasingly. She trusted Ted's judgement, and knew he cared for both of them.

Later that evening, Ted could see that Nicky couldn't wait to leg it out of the door over to the party.

"Go on then, it's 9.30 I reckon I can cope with the bar now that the restaurant is closed."

"Thank you, I will remember what you told me earlier, Cheers." Nicky left the pub and headed off to the party.

She walked up to Mick's house, and could hear the sound of U2 playing from the street. The track '*In a Little While*' was playing. She headed through the front door which was left ajar. Making her way through to the kitchen, she was greeted by a few locals lining the corridor on the way in. She found the host Mick in the kitchen. She was armed with half a dozen beers that she had bought from the pub. Mick was pouring a beer for one of his mates, he turned around and gave her one of his huge cheeky smiles.

"Hi there, pleased you could make it. Let me give you a hand with those beers."

"What can I get you to drink?"

"A glass of white would go down nicely please?" Nicky badly needed a drink for some Dutch courage. She added, I can only have one as I am driving later."

"You are welcome to crash here if you would like." Mick added, there are bound to be various bodies camping on the sofas later.

Nicky smiled and took the glass of wine.

*Mmmmm nice thought to stay the night. Will see how it goes.* Nicky thought as she headed out to catch the other guests.

"I will catch up with you in a while." Mick again gave Nicky a lovely smile and winked at her.

The evening was buzzing, and the party in full flow. Mick had offered Nicky a duvet if she wanted to stay. She had accepted and enjoyed a few more drinks and started to relax. She danced with the other gals and lads in the lounge, and got to know more about them. The party lasted well on into the early hours. They had stopped the music about half midnight, leaving just a few of them nattering well on into the morning.

"Shall I get your duvet?" Mick asked Nicky. Nicky looked at Mick, the couple had sat close to each other for the past hour or so, Mick had become very attentive towards her. He encouraged Nicky to follow him into his bedroom to collect her duvet. That was when the sparks flew, and they just couldn't keep their hands off each other. The passion was electric.

Mick whispered "Wait. I would like to play you some music." He walked over to his music system in his bedroom and chose a CD. Paloma Faith 'Fall To Grace."

Nicky couldn't risk his charm, along with the delightful sexy music. Exploring each other's bodies to the sound tracks which turned them both on. They giggled as they tried to stay silent with the other guests in close proximity.

"Don't worry about them, they are all pissed." Mick said encouraging Nicky into bed.

One to one is all they needed and they reached fulfilment together, and in time to the music track '*Let Your Love Walk In*'.

The alarm went off at 9am. Nicky rose first.

"I have to go, I need to collect Freddie from the kennels by 10."

Mick held her close, although he was well hung over, he was still needy.

"Come back later, I am not ready to let you go yet."

"I am working in the pub tonight again, come in later for a drink." Nicky left the house

That evening, Mick came into the pub looking very hung over.

"Hi Nicky, half a shandy please." Nicky laughed

"Here you go, that one is on me." She poured the drink

"Thank you for the lovely evening."

"It was all my pleasure, stay tonight again?" he added

"But I have Freddie." Nicky explained.

"Bring him too." Mick was adamant he wanted her to stay again.

Sometimes life moves too quickly. Nicky was scared she was going to be used as a stepping stone. But she couldn't help falling for him. Mick didn't realise how deeply she would fall. Within a week Nicky have moved in with Mick. They enjoyed a couple of raunchy months together. All seemed well until Mick suddenly got cold feet. Thing started to get very tricky. Nicky had problems with facing rejection. It had seemed so right. But now was going so so wrong.

Revenge is sweet, and when Mick asked Nicky to leave the house, she went into meltdown. She knew in her heart that he had gone cold on her. The arguments, being secretive about where he was going. It all took it's toll. Mick blocked her calls, and wanted to change the locks. Nicky managed some sweet revenge before he did. In floods of tears, she took a pint glass out of the kitchen stamped on it several times and put the broken glass in his bed between the sheets. She had heard in the pub that he had been seeing someone else. Mick had stayed away from the local. She left her keys on the table and a note "Arsehole!!!!"

She drove away from the flat with her beloved Freddie beside her and tears rolling down her cheeks. She had taken his Paloma Faith CD and played 'Never Tear Us Apart'.

Mick changed the locks; Nicky left the pub and moved back into Kingsbridge.

## Ten

Nicky enjoyed her job working at the Never Inn at Muckleigh just a few miles outside Kingsbridge in South Devon.

Saturdays were always a treat, with an early start of 10.30 in the mornings, running through until at least 10.30pm. Nicky would be given a short break during the afternoon before the evening session began. Being single, she could enjoy her social life in the pub, whilst earning some extra funds to finance the upkeep on her own horses.

Nicky owned a couple of thoroughbred horses, which she enjoyed riding. Owning a small piece of land of about four acres, she needed two horses for company. Her own competing days were over, but she still enjoyed the occasional day out hunting with the local harriers. One of her horses, Soloman, was an ex Point-to-Point racehorse, and he enjoyed a well-earned retirement of regular hacking and occasional hunting during the season.

Nicky really only went out hunting on Boxing Day and New Year's day. It would be difficult to help fund the horses if she chose to go out riding every Saturday, as these were her best earning days in the pub.

This Saturday was the last of the season. Nicky and the rest of the pub team knew that they were in for a busy day. It promised to be so busy, that Peter the landlord was worried that he had not ordered enough barrels of beer.

The day started with the usual pre-events drinks in the car park. The riders, supporters and locals would be out in force. Nicky ensured that the stirrup cup drinks (the welcome drink made up of rum punch) were filled and ready to hand around. She carried a tray out to the car park and started handing out the glasses. Amy offered up the tray to the riders, many of which she knew, and they thanked her.

When she came to the Huntsman, known as Eric, he asked

"Hi Nicky, why are you not out riding today?"

" Soloman lost a shoe, and to be honest, I could do with the money working here." Nicky smiled at Eric.

Nicky noticed that the black Irish Thoroughbred that Eric was sat on was immaculately turned out. So was Eric, in his fine hunting outfit. Eric was in his fourties, which was relatively young for a huntsman in a senior position.

Eric smiled at Nicky, and thanked her for the drink. "I look forward to catching up later in the bar then."

Nicky blushed and smiled back. She noticed that even with his riding hat on, he had a gorgeous lovely face and was a real gentleman. Eric was also really nice to his horse, who was fidgeting and wanted to get going and follow the drag scent.

Nicky carried on serving the drinks to all. She then headed back in the pub to collect some food, which had also been laid out on trays for all to enjoy. Mini pasties, sausage rolls and tiny sandwiches that Nicky had helped cut up herself too.

"Go go hurry up!" The landlord Peter was getting bossy.

"Yes I am on it." Replied Nicky, whilst thinking *Arsehole, get off my back, I don't want to drop this lot!*

The hunt set off at 11.30 and Nicky was soon back in the bar serving the locals who had come out to support the hunt. The bar was buzzing, and she really enjoyed the banter which was flying in her direction over the bar. She was a popular girl with the locals. A pretty brunette, with long hair, falling down to her waist. Having a tiny figure she could show it off nicely with some tight fitting clothes. She was tall enough to reach up to the optics, and wearing a cropped top, the lads would love a peek view of her tiny waist.

A good workout for barmaids too is pulling pints. It is something that builds up the arm muscles and helps keep them looking trim.

The afternoon soon whizzed by. The foot followers headed back to the pub at around 4.30pm.

"How far did they go?" asked Nicky

"The scent was laid all the way up to California Cross, and then back through the woods at Garabridge." Brian one of the followers said.

"What time will the horses be back?" Peter the landlord asked.

"About another hour I would guess, they were going back through Curtisknowle on the way hacking back."

"You can go for your break now Amy, if you can come back in an hour. There are lots of people eating tonight, so we will need you again."

Nicky headed off to see to her own animals. She had kept her horses in the stables, just in case the Hunt had headed through to Brownstown where her stables were. She wouldn't have wanted them excitably running around the fields wanting to join in with the hounds and horses following.

When Nicky arrived back at the pub, the hunt had already returned. Eric was washing down his horse in the yard behind the car park, he had been offered one of the stables to park the horse in until the following day. Eric knew he wouldn't be able to drive the lorry back after having a few pints, so had planned for a lift with the view to collecting the lorry and horse in the morning.

The bar was still buzzing. Mary had joined the evening bar session. She was great fun, a hoot with the locals with her outrageous clothing and fun banter. Both Nicky and Mary could run the bar well together. Peter and his wife Sandra would deal with the kitchen and restaurant side. Peter was an excellent cook, and served very good pub grub.

Nicky was pulling the pints, when suddenly the barrel had run out. She disappeared up the yard to where the beer cellar was. Attempting to untap the barrel, Nicky was struggling. She found it even more embarrassing as it was Eric the huntsman's pint she was trying to serve. She came back to the bar a bit flustered. Asking Mary:

"Can you un-tap this beer barrel for me? Peter is really busy in the kitchen, and I know he will snap my head off if I ask him."

"No. I don't know how." Mary replied

"I can tap it for you if you like?" Eric said. He followed Nicky up to the cellar.

Eric was still in his full hunting attire, and still looking immaculate. Nicky giggled.

"So sorry that you have to tap the barrel yourself to get your pint of beer."

"Don't worry, I can see it is really busy in the pub, so we wouldn't want to hassle Peter ."

Eric was checking out Nicky's cute butt as he followed her up the path to the cellar.

"It is in here, look I just can't tap it, maybe you can show me how?"

"Here you go, this is how you tap it." Just as Eric was hammering the tap into the barrel, there was an explosion of beer. It sprayed so much that it totally soaked Eric and all of his clothing.

Nicky looked on in dismay, she was mortified that Edward had soaked his beautiful clothes in beer. She was lucky to jump out of the way and missed most of the spray. Eric burst out laughing, and Nicky joined him.

"You are soaked!" claimed Nicky

"Yes help me out of these soaking clothes." Eric invited Nicky to undress him.

Even his hair was soaked. He looked at Nicky and she was beaming a smile which he just couldn't resist.

He kissed her passionately. Nicky was blown away with the situation, with Eric, and with the fact that they were being naughty in the cellar. What if Peter walked in? *Who cares* Nicky thought!

With his jacket and shirt off, Eric looked even more desirable. The couple had a passionate five minutes over the barrel. Intense passion that fulfilled both of them.

"We had better get back to the bar quick." Nicky knew Mary would start to get inquisitive, even if Peter was distracted with the food orders. People would be queuing for the beer.

They walked back into the bar. Eric had his jacket thrown over his shoulder.

"What on earth has happened to you Eric?" Mary asked.

Nicky was giggling, both she and Eric were like naughty teenagers.

"Well I thought I knew how to tap the barrel, but it was obviously well loaded and exploded over both of us. " Eric smiled

"Let's pour you that well deserved pint now Eric." Nicky blushed as she poured the pint and passed it to Eric.

"Yes I have suddenly got a thirst on, and need that one." Eric chuckled at Nicky and turned to join the rest of the riders.

"You took your time up in the cellar, what did you two get up to? That new Huntsman is a bit of a dish!" Mary raised her eyebrows at Nicky.

"That would be telling." Replied Nicky tapping her nose but grinning at the same time.

# Should It Happen To A Barmaid?

## *Eleven*

Barmaids come in all shapes and sizes, but this chapter is about a lucky 6ft tall, leggy, blonde babe called Lisa who worked at the local football club namely Plymouth Athletico.

Lisa was born and bred in Plymouth, her Daddy was a local property developer, and he was one of the trustees of the club. Lisa herself was enjoying a gap year from university. Having qualified as a beauty therapist, she had taken some time to travel the world, before settling down to open up her own salon which her father would be funding. She was far from a spoilt child, and like her father, she was prepared to work hard for a living.

Her father, Graham, had found Lisa some work in the club bar. She had been recently jilted by her then boyfriend who she met on her travels, and needed a distraction.

Lisa was absolutely gorgeous; she had the majority of men falling at her feet. Not only the team players, but the clubs trustee's and hundreds of the loyal supporters. The club bar had become a much busier place with Lisa there to cheer them all up. Lisa was a breath of fresh air behind the bar. Being well travelled, and full of enthusiasm for life, she could cheer up anyone who had a bad day.

Kevin, the team manager, was one such person who was having a bad day. He had come in fresh from the dressing room. Once again the team had performed badly. They were facing relegation. This had a knock on effect with all involved in the club. They were all worried about their jobs. If the team were relegated into the league below, then there would be less money in the pot to go around, with job cuts being inevitable.

Despite being very spoilt, Lisa was very attentive as to what was happening around her. She would easily pick up on vibes around her, and was a very good listener. She would be equally comfortable listening to the chaps as well as the ladies drinking in the bar. Although the majority, in this case, were male.

It had been the first play-off match of the season. The team had to win to secure their place in the league. The supporters had been loyal, but their dedication was starting to wear thin. They were starting to get frustrated with the lack of goals, and having just been defeated 3-1 were jeered off the pitch. Kevin the manager was under enormous pressure. He had been manager of the club for ten years, and this was their worst season ever. It was becoming a slippery slope to an inevitable loosing end. The recession had played its part, with Kevin struggling to attract good players with the limited funds on offer.

After the game, Kevin had his usual pep talk with his players in the dressing room. He had to give the players a stiff talking to. He had left them in the changing room with plenty to dwell on. He headed to the bar, and took his usual seat in the corner.

"Southern Comfort and Coke please. Actually make it a double."

Lisa poured his drink and looked Kevin directly into his eyes

"Bad day/" she asked, knowing the team had lost, but not letting on how much it meant to Kevin and his team.

"Yes, we have to win next week, otherwise we drop a league, and I will probably loose my job."

Lisa knew her place behind the bar was to look after the drinkers, help the teams celebrate their wins or commiserate their losses and the consequences that result had on them. The team lads like to watch the replays when they came into the bar. Kevin had left them in the changing room to contemplate the game and their 3-1 home defeat. He has to be tough, and take off any player who is not joining in or contributing to the best of their ability.

This in turn can make Kevin unpopular as a manager. He has to name and shame, for the sake of the other players who put their all in. They all knew who the weakest links were. The players who didn't perform would also be on a downer. It was their reputation and job on the line too.

It can often be an awkward moment for Lisa, when the loosing team walked into the bar. If they had done badly both Lisa and the other barmaids knew it would be a challenge to lift them up and get them to think positive again. Lisa knew that the odds were stacked against Kevin, it would be a miracle if he could turn it around now.

"Four pints of Doombar please?" asked one of the players.

The lads had slowly started to make their way out of the changing rooms and order their first beers.

"Next week will be better." Lisa smiled at the lads

They couldn't help but smile back, although it was usually the last lot that walked through from the changing rooms that knew they were destined for the transfer list if they didn't improve pretty damn quick!

"You better make the most of tonight's drinks lads. No beer until after the next game." shouted Kevin

Lisa knew that the lads would be on a mission, to drown their sorrows and down a few pints before the drinking curfew kicked in. Many of the team abstained from alcohol during the season. But then with pressure on and men being men, a few pints after a match seemed acceptable.

"Another Southern Comfort please Lisa." asked Kevin

The bar was becoming livelier now the lads had downed their first pints, and were relaxing nicely. Various comments would fly around the bar during the replay as to who had and hadn't performed. Humiliation was inevitable. Hopefully they would leave their mistakes behind, and come back a stronger team next week.

Lisa noticed that Kevin was downing a few Southern Comforts. He looked troubled. A very worried man. *Having a family to support can't be easy*. Lisa thought. She tried hard to cheer him up. Funds in the team had been dipping with the lack of supporters through the gate. They couldn't afford to buy better players.

"The jeering and slow clapping at the end of the game is getting to me. I am not sure I can handle it much longer. I am pleased it is coming up to the end of the season. I just want to run away."

Lisa studied Kevin's face. Being a qualified beautician she admired a good facial profile. Behind all that wear Kevin was a good looking chap. He was in his early fifties. Lisa was in her twenties, but the age gap didn't seem to matter to her. Kevin had a certain something about him, a maturity and kind nature that attracted Lisa to him. Kevin himself had been a football player, and still liked to keep his body fit. But the stress of facing imminent relegation was starting to wear him down. Kevin was looking drawn and depressed.

The team players would always flirt with Lisa, but she personally preferred the older chap. Often finding the younger lads a bit immature and very cocky. Footballers they were, but also players in love. Many women would be falling at their feet, they had a choice of several, and would be determined to play the field before settling down. Kevin was married, although not happily, but with two teenage children who would sometimes come along to the games.

"I am sure next weekend will be better." Lisa spoke reassuringly to Kevin.

Many of the players had their fill of pints and had started to leave the club. The loyal players were keen to keep control of their lives and hopefully do their manager proud next weekend. It was still possible they could stay in the league, but had to win the game, otherwise it was definite relegation.

Lisa changed the music in the CD system and chose the album Blessed Union of the Soul. Kevin had decided to grab a taxi home, but before he did he asked

"One for the road please." and held out his glass for a

refill. He added "My wife has no time for me, she thinks I am a failure, but she is happy to go out on spending sprees when it suits her though."

"It is not just you, it is the whole team." Replied Lisa

"Yes but I should have made changes earlier on in the season, when some of the players started to play poorly. I should have substituted them."

Lisa was lending a sympathetic ear, and Kevin was keen to offload on her whilst supping his last Southern Comfort.

"I am not sure what will happen, how I can afford to pay the kids school fees. They are both at private school and at a venerable age."

"Maybe you should send Debbie out to work."

Kevin chuckled

"That's not an option, she hasn't done a decent days work in her life! She will leave me I know, but at this moment I don't care." Kevin was getting upset.

Lisa noticed a tear running down his cheek. She touched his hand and he looked up at her.

"I need a miracle, to turn this team around." Kevin wiped the tear from his face.

Lisa was alone in the bar with Kevin. She wanted to hug him. She was a natural giver. Appreciating the way her father had bought her up. Into a wealthy family, but she had worked hard to obtain her qualification and was prepared to take on jobs to earn her pocket money.

It was Lisa's job to lock up the bar and hand the keys to the groundkeeper before she left. Lisa didn't hurry Kevin to drink up.

"I need to get my bag and jacket out of the changing rooms." Said Kevin

Lisa followed him saying "I have always been interested to see the changing rooms."

"Fancy a Sauna?" Kevin asked cheekily.

Lisa had a look in the door, then turned to Kevin and squeezed his arm reassuringly.

"Are you going to be OK?"

Kevin looked at Lisa, she was beautiful and he was enjoying her company. He sat on the bench in the sauna. Lisa joined Kevin sitting over him and gave him a passionate kiss.

"Lovely distraction, thank you Lisa."

He put his hand up to her face, pausing before kissing her. The sauna was not on, but the atmosphere was hot enough and turned them both on. Lisa gave Kevin some intimate TLC. He has said that his marriage was rocky, and that his wife was only interested in shopping on his hard earned earnings. Lisa had nothing to loose, she was a giver, and gave her body and soul to Kevin that evening.

It was exactly what Kevin had needed. Lisa could feel the urgency in his body and his desire to make her happy too.

The team had a training session every day before the big match. The lads looked happier and Kevin was much more positive. The positivity had shown through and the team started to gel again. All hopes were on Saturday's match.

It was an away game, meaning even more pressure with loyal fans paying more on travelling to the game some 200 miles away in Coventry.

Kevin and Lisa had text contact during the week. Lisa wasn't looking for a long term relationship and certainly not one with someone thirty years her senior. She did appreciate Kevin thanking her for an amazing sauna room session.

The Plymouth team won the match on Saturday and avoided relegation. The club bar was opened on Sunday lunchtime for the team to celebrate. The players and members enjoyed a few hours of a champagne reception laid on for them. Kevin was happy to keep his manager job, and now being more positive with a better attitude, he wanted to stay another season.

He and Lisa exchanged a glance across the bar. He then texted her.

"I CAN NEVER THANK YOU ENOUGH! xxx

## Should It Happen To A Barmaid?

### *Twelve*

Lisa had managed to get an interview for a barmaid job in one of the Naval bars in Plymouth,

"What shall I wear for the interview?" she asked her friend Claire.

"Something smart and sexy, you will be interviewed by one of the Navel Officers. I understand it is quite a strict selection process." replied Claire.

"Ok, I will wear my short navy blue skirt and a tidy sexy top. Shall we meet up for coffee after?"

"Yes I would love to hear how you get on. Let's meet for coffee at about 4pm?"

"Deal, see you later Claire."

Lisa was excited about the interview. She had been single for some time. Her last boyfriend cheated on her. She had got very fond of Chris her ex. However Chris had other ideas being a good looking chap, he often had women falling at his feet. Lisa was of the attitude that it just wasn't meant to be and had moved on. It was just as well they had split up then, than stick together any longer and he be fickle enough to run off with another woman in a few years time.

Lisa arrived at the officer's mess at 2.20pm, her interview was at 2.30pm. She thought that it would bode well if she arrived early.

"Mr Gold will see you now if you would like to follow me?" Katie the receptionist smiled at Lisa, she added

"Don't worry, he is very friendly, just looks a bit official in his uniform."

"This is Lisa Wild, Lisa this is Mr Gold."

"Thank you Katie." Replied Mr Gold

Lisa noticed that Mr Gold looked very tasty wearing his Naval Officers uniform. He had short cropped blond hair and simmering blue eyes. He stood up and held out his hand to greet her.

"Hello." Said Lisa shaking his hand and melting into his eyes.

"Now Lisa, please take a seat." Mr Gold sat down on the other side of the desk.

"I have taken a look through your C.V. and you have been short listed for our vacancy in the bar. But I have to warn you Lisa, the Naval lads can be quite exceptionally naughty and badly behaved when they head back from months at sea." He continued

"We need staff who can be discrete, as it's not the easiest bar job in the world. You will have to be open minded."

"I have worked in university and football bars before, I am sure I could handle it." replied Lisa.

"My name is Edward, please call me that."

"If that is ok then I will Mr Gold, oh I mean Edward." Lisa giggled and held his gaze.

"I must also warn you Lisa that there is an element of nudity in the bar at times, the lads run ashore is very wild!"

Lisa blushed and replied

"I think I can handle that."

"Good, we do have a number of chaps who will stay on duty to police the situation, you will not be in any danger."

"That is handy to know, I am not sure I am up for an open orgy!" Lisa chuckled.

"Good, can I ring you and let you know if you have been successful with the job? I still have a few others to interview." Edward stood up and moved towards the door.

Lisa stood up "Yes of course, you have my number"

"I will ring you in the next couple of days Lisa, thank you for coming." Edward shook Lisa's hand and again she melted into his eyes.

"How did it go?" asked Katie the receptionist as Lisa walked through to leave.

"Hopefully well." replied Lisa crossing her fingers.

Lisa sent Claire a text. CAN'T WAIT TO TELL YOU ABOUT INTERVIEW, ON MY WAY TO CAFÉ ROUGE.

Claire replied. GREAT SEE YOU THERE IN A BIT

Lisa bounced into Café Rouge to find Claire already sitting at one of the tables.

"What can I get you? Coffee or wine? You look excited!"

"A glass of wine would go down nicely please. Edward Gold the Naval Officer was gorgeous. Hope I get the job!"

"I am sure you will, you would be a great asset to any bar." beamed Claire as she went to order the drinks.

"I hope so, I would love to meet Edward Gold again, let alone work in the bar with the rest of the Naval chaps."

"Edward did pre warn me of what naughtiness goes on when the lads arrive back on shore, he warned me to be open minded."

"So its Edward is it? First name terms already. It will be a new chapter in your life Lisa, you deserve a decent time now." Giggles Claire

"I so hope I get the job." Lisa sipped her wine.

Lisa only had to wait a day before Edward Gold was on the phone to her.

"We would like to offer you the job Lisa, I think you will be a good barmaid for us. I have checked your with references and they have both given you a glowing report. Would you like to come in Friday evening? We have a ship due back in to port during the day, so the bar will be very busy in the evening, and we could do with the extra help."

"Yes I accept." replied Lisa, who could hardly squeak her words out.

"Good, see you at 7pm sharp Lisa."

"Thank you, bye, see you then." Lisa put down the phoned and squealed with delight. She phoned Claire

"I've got the job, Edward just phoned me!"

"Great I knew you would, well done you. You will get to see Mr Gold again. When do you start?"

"Friday night, Edward said it would be busy as there is a ship due back in that day. I need to get some early nights before then."

"You will be fine, what are you going to wear?"

Lisa replied "My short blue dress, you know the one that's low cut in front. I want to keep the navy blue theme."

"Well if you don't pull then, you never will, even if it's not Mr lush Gold, the boys won't be able to resist you!"

"That's the plan." replied Lisa

Friday evening soon arrived and Lisa had taken an hour to get ready, shower, sort out her hair, make up and dressing to her best for the Naval bar. The thought of working in a bar serving over 300 mostly male Naval drinkers promised to be a delight, and what girl wouldn't look forward to that job? *Let's hope they don't get riotous!* Lisa thought.

She arrived at the bar just before seven to be greeted by a

couple of uniformed Naval Officers at the bar.

"Hi you must be Lisa the new barmaid." asked one of the chaps.

"Yes, how did you guess?" Lisa asked inquisitively

"You fit the description well!" laughed one of the chaps teasingly

"Carl will introduce you to the other barmaids if you follow him in. But please sign the staff register first."

"Yes of course, no problem." Lisa signed the book

As she was led through to the bar, she noted the music playing Jack Savoretti's album Written in Scars, she loved the music and immediately relaxed. She was introduced to the five other barmaids and two smart young barmen; they all made Julie feel welcome. There were two bars situated either side of the huge room, which was like a military base. With up to 300 drinkers expected, the team behind the bar would be kept busy.

Natalie, one of the other barmaids took Lisa under her wing and showed her how the till worked and the drinks on offer. Lisa was well used to pouring shorts as well as pints, so it didn't take her long to feel at home.

"How many bars have you worked in?" asked Natalie

"A few, one at University and then the football club bar, but no military or naval bars before."

"Well you will love this one and be in for a real treat if you are open minded, the boys are normally well behaved. They just like to have fun and play silly games, which you can understand with them being at sea for months defending our country."

"I look forward to witnessing that later." Lisa laughed with Claire.

The lads started to file into the bar. Groups of seven or eight at a time, which was manageable for the bar staff. Once they had arrived back in port, many had met up with their wives and families, but it was a tradition for many of them to stay and party before settling back into home life having found their land legs again.

*They just keep coming through the door.* Lisa thought as one hunky chap after another kept filing through. *Jeeezes I am in heaven!!*

There was a great atmosphere. Lisa was loving the job.

"Haven't seen you here before, are you new?" one of the chaps asked.

"It's my first day." Lisa replied whilst grinning from ear to ear.

"Hope you are ready for a fun party!" the lad winked and headed off with his pints of larger to the rest of his group of mates.

She then spotted Edward Gold, he walked through the door still wearing a uniform. Her heart jumped a beat. He caught Lisa's eye and walked over to her.

"Would you like a drink Mr Gold?" she didn't think it appropriate to call him Edward in front of the other bar staff.

"No I am on duty, just wanted to check that you were settling in ok? I need to alert the bouncers if there is any trouble brewing, but I see the chaps are behaving."

"Yes thank you I am enjoying it so far."

With that one of the chaps jumped on a table and shouted "Naked bar."

To Lisa's amazement all of the drinking chaps stripped off totally naked. Julie blushed.

"Don't worry." Edward turned to Lisa and could sense her embarrassment. "I didn't want to tell you too much before, as I didn't want to put you off coming to work here. They are pretty harmless really."

Lisa giggled as she didn't know where to look, but focused on the lovely Graham Gold, the other bar staff were laughing and just got on pulling pints.

The lads supped their pints and put some of their clothes back on. But not before she noticed how muscular many were. There were a few who were playing games with their pint glasses. As the night wore on and they were getting more drunk, some would be playing spoofing games. Spoof is a game where a group of people have a number of coins each in their hands. Usually three coins are held, but they can grasp in their hands either one two or three coins. The group then play a game as to who can guess the total number of coins held within the group. With the loser having to play a forfeit. In this instance the forfeit was whatever disgusting liquid they had poured into the glass. Urine and other bodily fluids were the forfeit in this bar.

*Yuk!* Lisa thought.

"The lads are harmless really, it is their way of maintaining their sanity after months at sea." Edward again explained to Lisa to put her at ease.

Lisa was game tho, and enjoyed the evening. The barmaids were paid bonuses if they kept quiet about what went on, especially when the lads were bringing their wives or girlfriends back into the bar the following week. Many of the chaps were extremely fit, and they must have been working out in the gym on the ship to keep their bodily physique. The lads were posers and they were sure going to show their bodies off.

# Should It Happen To A Barmaid?

## *Thirteen*

In the popular tourist seaside resort of Torquay, Julie had landed herself a job in one of the clubs there called The Domino. Staff are chosen for their bubbly personalities. Fun loving gals and guys were important to keep the club going.

This club is definitely not a club for the barmaid who preferred a quiet night serving beer to the locals whilst discussing the daily crossword which appears in the paper. Attracting both locals and holiday makers, it had become one of the most popular clubs in town.

Gary and James are the resident bouncers at the Domino Club. Stocky fit chaps who could break up a fight easily, and just the look of them would make any trouble maker think twice about causing trouble. Their job was to check out anyone who entered the premises, and that all who entered to enjoy the fun. Until everyone had left the premises in an orderly manner.

This club was right up Julie's street. She intended to enjoy every minute of it. The policy of the club was to employ all female staff. The landlord Charlie had an eye for the ladies, and he managed to attract some beauties to work for him.

Julie herself was in her mid-forties She had kept herself

fit and attended the local gym for swimming and to use the apparatus to help keep her figure. She had a tiny waist and loved to show it off.

Julie arrived for her barmaid duty.

"Lovely outfit!" James the bouncer commented on Julie's crop top T-shirt, which enhanced her tiny waist.

"Why thank you James, I intend to have fun tonight."

Julie was also one of the bar managers, being of the older generation, up to 20 years older than some of the younger staff working there. She looked after the younger girls. Still fit for her age, Julie or Jules as she like to be called, could still pull the chaps, any age from 18 to over 60. They were taken in by her vivacious manner. She would be at the bar with the chaps lapping at her feet.

James commented to his fellow bouncer Gary

"She is looking to pull tonight, let's have £20 guessing who she will leave with."

Gary laughed "She is pretty fussy, it will cost them dear, as she doesn't come cheap! Ok £20 it is."

"Deal" said James and the bouncers shook hands
As the club goers flocked through the door, the bouncers had fun guessing whom Jules would get off with.

"Found your winner yet James?" asked Gary

"No the night is young yet. Jules will be keeping us guessing for a while, she is a bit of a tart and will give many the come on!"

The boys were right as one after one they witnessed various men chatting Jules up at the bar. She was a real man magnet and great business for the club. Many of the chaps would offer her a drink, she would always accept, and kept a tab running. The barmaids also had their own little competition as to who they could pull on the night. There was a limit to how many drinks the barmaids were allowed to consume during the evening, so they would run up tabs lists and tot up who was the winner at the end of the evening. Jules would always have the longest list. The club owner Charlie would treat each night's winner to a steak, to encourage the girls to be very flirty with the customers.

On this particular night, the club had put on an open Mic night. These nights proved very popular, as people would flock to see any hidden raw musical talent that might turn up to try their first taste of singing in front of an audience. A few talented holiday guests would also try their luck too.

Jules caught the attention of one of the fathers accompanying his 18 year old son. Jack had stunning raw sound to his voice. His father Brian accompanied him to many pub open mic nights, hoping that Jack would get talent spotted. He and his father were staying locally for the weekend, they had managed to find a B & B and had heard of the Club whilst staying there. Jack always took his guitar wherever he went.

Brian walked up to the bar to where Jules was serving.

"What can I get you to drink?" Jules asked

"Pint of Cidre for me please, and a pint of orange squash for my son Jack."

"Coming up, are you local?"

"No we are down for the weekend from Kent, my son is keen on open Mic nights."

" Great, I can't wait to hear him sing."

"He has a lovely voice, but them I am biased being his father I guess. Would you like a drink?" Brian asked

"Yes please, I will have a Gin and tonic with you please." Jules took Brian's money and wrote her drink on the tab.

The singers had started to play their music. They were well received with lots of clapping and whistling. Brian headed back up to the bar for another drink.

"Another Cidre and a pint of orange squash please." Brian asked Jules again.

"What music does Jack sing?" Julie loved her music and was always keen to support young talent.

"He sings with a guitar, lots of Van Morrison, Brian Adams, and newer artists such as James Bay and Jack Savoretti."

"Husky voice then? That will be £6.20 for the drinks please?"

"Would you like another?" Brian offered Jules a £10 note.

"Yes pls why thank you. That will be the straight tenner then." Jules clocked up another drink on her tab

Gary had clocked Jules talking to Brian.

"Hey up, think the £20 bet may be mine, I guessed that one walking through the door" Gary said to James

"I am not so sure, he has his son with him, she would have to get him to send his son home on his own if she ends up with him, I think they are holiday makers."

"Maybe you are right, we had better keep guessing." James was looking around the club for another suitable candidate.

Both the bouncers headed back out to the doors. Happy to think that the crowd in the bar were behaving themselves. It was past 11pm and the streets were starting to build up with the  pubs kicking out. Many would que up for the clubs.

"Here, what about this chap walking in now?" James suggested

A middle aged tall dark gentleman was taking his line in the que along with some of his mates. He looked to be about fifty, and was wearing smart jeans and a red checked shirt.

"Think the £20 is mine. He has settled himself at the end of the bar and has just bought Jules a drink." James was talking to Gary through his ear piece, James was checking the crowd inside, and Gary was left manning the door.

"Are you local?" Jules inquired to the handsome chap that was sat at her end of the bar.

"No, I am delivering a boat down to Plymouth, I have just sailed from the Hamble." The chap was very good looking and was glowing with the sea air he had been in all day."

"Nice weather for sailing. What type of boat?" asked Jules

"It's a Jenneau 32, she is a nice cruising boat. Has been bought by a couple in Plymouth for some coastal cruising."

"What's your name?" Jules was keen to find out more.

"Roger, I do lots of boat deliveries. Would you like a drink?"

"Yes please, my name is Jules. Nice to meet you,." Jules offered Roger her hand to shake over the bar.

Roger stayed at the end of the bar for the rest of the night. He had bought Jules six drinks that evening. Jules had drunk two of them and written the rest down on her tab.

Jules and Roger left the club together.

"She is a cheeky monkey" Gary said to James," Have you seen the comments she has made on her tab behind the bar?"

James replied "Well I won the £20 bet between us, but what does it say?"

"She has listed all the drinks down, made comments and scored the chaps. She has gone off with the chap who has bought her the most drinks over the evening!" Gary laughed

Jules and Roger spent a night of passion on the boat together.

# Should It Happen To A Barmaid?

## *Fourteen*

In the summer of 2015, Julie was working as a Barmaid in the Old Inn pub, near Totnes in Devon. The pub was popular with travellers, being situated close to the main route from Kingsbridge to Totnes some 15 miles from Plymouth. Many businessmen travelling from Plymouth via Kingsbridge, would use the Bed and Breakfast facilities that the pub offered. Together with decent pub grub, it became an ideal location to stop in.

Visitors come and visitors go. Julie found the pub work interesting, and loved to meet new people. Coming from the East coast, she was well travelled herself.

A group of chaps walked into the bar.

"Hi we have three rooms booked for tonight."

"Ok what names are they booked under please?" asked Julie

"Mark Sutton, Graham Riley and Steve Horton."

"Yes I have found your booking. I will show you to your rooms." Julie smiled and led the chaps upstairs.

The pub only had three letting rooms. It was an Olde world type pub that had been used as an Inn for centuries.

If only walls had ears, there would be plenty of stories to tell.

Mark was South African, a rather large chap standing over six foot tall, with the broadest shoulders Julie had ever seen. The other two chaps Graham and Steve were slight build, medium height and unremarkable looking.

"You had better have this room, it is the largest one we have." Julie showed Mark into his room. She then showed the other two chaps into their rooms.

"Are you only staying the one night?" Julie asked them

Mark replied. "Yes, we have come down to go spearfishing in Dartmouth, they have no rooms left in the town, so we thought this was the next best option."

"Dinner is served from 6.30pm, the bar is open all day and closes at 11pm."

"Thank you." Mark said as he looked Julie in the eyes with a captivating stare.

Julie left the chaps to sort out their gear and went back down to the bar.

*Interesting chaps Julie thought!*

Mark and his friends, Steve and Graham, freshened up in their room and headed down to the bar. They were looking at the menu when Julie asked

"Are you chaps hungry? I can recommend the steak."

"May we have three T-Bones please?"

"Yes, how would you like them cooked Sir?"

"Two medium rare and one rare please." Mark spoke for them all

*I bet he is having the rare one, he looks a bit like an animal!* Julie thought.

Julie was captivated by Mark's handsome face. Not normally her type, but something, just something attracted her to him. He was very masculine. *Maybe a rugby player?* She thought.

Mark came up to the bar and ordered three pints of Doombar. They were sat over in the corner table.

"Shall I bring the pints over?" Julie was trying to be helpful, and keen at the same time.

"Yes please that's kind of you."

After delivering the beer, Julie took the food order up to the kitchen.

"I will take their steaks out when they are ready." Julie was keen to look after that table.

"Ah who has taken your fancy then Julie." Mary the landlady asked.

"The group of chaps who have booked in as residents. The South African chap is real fit!" Julie chucked.

Mark came up to the bar for another beer order.

"What do you do when you are not spearfishing?" Julie was intrigued.

"I am a medical rep, I work for a company in Bristol. I have been down here on holiday before, but this is the first time spearfishing."

"What exactly is spearfishing?" Julie inquired

"It is fishing, by swimming with a snorkel and a spear. Not like normal fishing with a rod." Mark added "Do you live local?"

"Yes, I live in the village here."

Their food order was ready and Julie took out their plates of scrumptious food.

"Mmmm that looks very tasty!" commented Graham

"Enjoy your food gentleman." Julie left them to eat.

She walked back up to the kitchen.

"Oh my Oh my, they are fit!!!"

"Dare you to get off with South African Chap." Mary the

chef teased Julie

It was St Patricks day, and Julie being Irish was in a good mood, and having a few drinks. She was up for a challenge so agreed.

"Now there's an idea, I am up for a challenge." Julie headed back to the bar.

The chaps had finished their food. She went over to the table.

"Can I offer you dessert?"

Mark looked at Julie, he looked her up and down and said

"That depends what you have on offer?"

"Behave now!" Julie laughed and added "I will bring over the dessert menu for you."

"Can we have three more pints too please, and have one for yourself too."

"Ok and thank you I will."

Julie enjoyed the banter in the pub more than ever that evening. The spearfishermen were good fun, apparently it was a sport that was becoming ever more popular with the warmer sea waters around South Devon.

The lads were downing the drinks and keeping Julie

topped up too. Mary the landlady came out of the kitchen at about 10pm.

"You can clock off now Julie, thanks for looking after the place, I know we are a bit short staffed, and I do appreciate your efforts."

Julie was having too much fun to go home, and joined the chaps for more booze. She was getting well drunk. There were a few other local fishermen in the pub that night, together with the normal local crowd it was the place to be. She was getting on very well with Mark, so much so that she was sat beside him flirting away. Both were getting very 'touchy feely.'

For Julie it was a bet, which she had with Mary, so when Mark invited her up to his room she thought she had nothing to loose. Mark bought a bottle of wine from the bar and the two headed up stairs. Steve and Graham stayed in the bar for last orders. Julie put the thumbs up to Mary, as they headed up the stairs with Mark.

Once in the room, Mark poured some wine.

"I am not sure I need much more drink" Julie stated.

The couple had a quick passionate kiss and cuddle. They got very heated very quickly, undressing each other. Mark got up to put on the TV to play some music and tuned into the music channel. Julie looked at him from the bed. *Oh my God!* She thought as she caught a glimpse of his profile from behind. She had a cough and looked again, thinking that maybe the booze had something to do with it. But she had seen his masculinity dangling between his legs. It was dangling down to his knees.

"My god she said, where do you think you are going to put that."

Mark turned to face her and she fainted.

He lay on the bed beside her and trickled some wine onto her lips. She came round to Mark trickling wine over her body whilst following through with his tongue.

Mark whispered "Don't worry I will be gentle, it will fit, believe me."

Julie responded to Mark's caressing.

She woke in the morning and the bed beside her was empty. There was a note left on the side table saying 'Thanks very much, hope you had as much fun as I did. Mark'

Julie wondered *Did we or didn't we?* Then she started to remember, she gingerly got out of bed and made her way to the bathroom. *Where are my knickers? I think he has run off with them!!!??* Naturally she was sore, but managed to pee ok.

It was Julie's job to clean the rooms. She checked the time, it was 8.30am. She managed to make it down the stairs to find Mary clearing up in the kitchen after breakfast. Mary looked at Julie and laughed.

"You put me up to that! I shouldn't have taken the bet on. You should have seen the size of his manhood!"

Mary chuckled, well by the way you are walking you obviously had a good night!"

"I fainted whilst he was putting some music on the tv channel. I came round as he was caressing me, and got swept away with the moment. And I think he has run off my knickers as a trophy the bugger!"

"Do you want me to do the changeover on the rooms are are you ok to make it back up the stairs?" Mary asked sympathetically.

"It's ok, I will do it, that's what I am paid for." And Julie went back upstairs chuntering to herself.

She did Mark's room first, as she wanted to double check for her knickers, but still couldn't find them. She then managed to do Grahams room. When she got to Steve's room and stripped off the bed she couldn't believe her eyes, as her pair of knickers were in Steve's bed. *Oh no what else did I get up to last night!!!*

Julie was good friends with the landlady Mary, and when Julie managed to hobble down the stairs she looked for Mary.

"You found them where?!" Mary was shocked.

"I can't believe I had both of them? Maybe the third one joined in too.!"

"Don't worry Mary said supportively, they probably did it as a joke. You go home and have a nice soak in the bath."

"Ok, see you tomorrow." Julie hobbled of home muttering to herself.

# Should It Happen To A Barmaid?

## *Fifteen*

The annual young farmers dance was a real treat for the local farmer lads to catch up at the end of the summer harvest. Held in September each year, after the majority of the crops have been harvested, and only a few weeks of third cut silaging grass cutting left to do.

Ben was one of the local young farmers who was particularly looking forward to the end of harvest bash. His father being the land owner where the event was to be held. Having worked hard all summer, Ben had been one of the tractor drivers, working from dawn until dusk to get the land prepared, crops sown and harvested to feed the cattle on their farm and supply corn for the food trade.

Ben loved to socialise, and on his rare few nights off, had frequented the local pub to have a few glasses of his favourite drink, Guinness. He also had his eagle eye on one of the new barmaids in the local pub. He would sit for hours at the end of the bar letching at Bridget. Ben would buy her drinks, flashing his cash, and chat her up.

Bridget was a good listener; she was a young, lively, blonde barmaid, with short cropped hair. Her figure was slightly stocky, but that didn't bother Ben, he knew that she was a farrier by trade, and needed to be strong enough to pick up horses legs for hours on end whilst shoeing them.

Ben was so taken with Bridget that he would neglect his mates to chat her up. Every time he would head to the pub, he made sure that he showered and changed and wore his favourite aftershave for Bridget. She would be a listening ear for him, ask him about his day, and share in his highs and lows.

Ben once had a childhood sweetheart called Debbie. It didn't last, as both were young, and Ben being committed to the farm, their romance just fizzled out before it got started. Debbie went off to college, and the romance ended.

Ben became besotted with Bridget. He idolised her. Bridget knew how to pour a pint of Guinness, which was Ben's favourite tipple, and she would tease him by doing artwork on the top of his pint, well so he thought.

"Hi Ben, Guinness for you?"

Bridget would have the glass ready as Ben walked into the bar. Ben thought it was because he was special, but Bridget just knew her job, and knew exactly what each and every customer wanted as soon as they appeared. Although she always asked them, just in case they had a different appetite that evening.

"Yes please Bridget." Ben was always smiling when he caught sight of Bridget, together with the anticipation of tasting his first pint, for him it was heaven.

"Have you had a good day Ben?" Bridget knew that Ben spent hours on his tractor working on the land, ploughing the fields, seeding and harvesting the land."

"Yes, finished the last of the silage today, and the big bale hayledge too. It's been a very good harvest."

Farmers need the weather right to be able to produce a bumper crop. Too wet and they can't get on the land, too dry and the crops and grass doesn't grow. Farming is a fine art. Farmers have to be totally dedicated with 24/7 round the clock working hours. Many have never had a day's sick in their lifetime. The work has to be done otherwise they do not earn any money. Animals have to be fed and watered to survive.

Bridget enjoyed working in a rural area, she soon got to know the local drinkers and eaters who used the pub. She enjoyed Ben's company when he came in for his pints of Guinness. She felt sorry for him. Ben's father was well into his seventies, and Ben was young to take on such a responsibility of running the farm. He was taking on more and more pressure. Bridget would always have time for Ben and asked him how his day had gone, offering him a cheery smile.

For generations farmers have found themselves a wife, either through going out to the local pub, or at the end of season young farmer's events. Earthy people who care for their animals, and could potentially care for them, the bread earners. The farmer wants a wife, and he wants to be looked after in a proper manner. Someone to feed, care for him and to raise his family.

Bridget seemed to fit the bill for Ben. She was fun,

attractive to him, and held good conversation. She also had started her own business as a farrier. She came from a farming family herself. *Ideal for me!* Ben thought.

"The young farmers party is on next weekend, it is being held on our farm, are you going? Ben asked Bridget.

"Yes I am helping behind the bar for a few hours. Bob the landlord has asked me."

Ben knew that Bob the Landlord was supplying the booze for the evening; he had hoped that Bridget would be there.

"Great." Ben's plan was to get Bridget to dance with him. The event was to be held on Ben's parents' 150 acre farm, which was an ideal location for pitching a Marquee.

"The Marquee arrives on Thursday, I have kept that field free of sheep so that the ladies do not spoil their shoes." Laughed Ben

Bridget laughed too "Yes it can be a bit off putting, what music do you have?"

"Mad Dog Macrea." Replied Ben

"They are brilliant." agreed Bridget and added "How many people are you expecting?"

"About 300 we hope, it's also a fund raising evening for Devon Air Ambulance, so we hope to raise funds on the evening."

Ben was finding his Guinness refreshing and ordered another. He also offered Bridget a drink. He was fairly wealthy, having worked hard and being the only son an heir to the estate. He thought that maybe if he flashed his cash around he could attract Bridget.

Bridget found Ben fun, but she wasn't that attracted to him. That didn't stop Ben from trying his hardest. Maybe once Bridget had seen his beautiful Devon farm she may be drawn to him. Bridget was single, so Ben thought he must be in with a chance. *Maybe she just hasn't found the right chap?*

There are only a few female farriers in the country, and Ben admired her for doing a tough job. She had finished her apprenticeship and had started to get a good following of clients. She took on a few nights Barmaiding at the pub to help fund buying a new truck for her work. Many yards in Devon were off road, where a 4WD vehicle was a must, but they didn't come cheap.

The day before the Young Farmers dance Ben bounded into the pub.

"Guinness?" Bridget asked

"Yes please, the Marquee is looking great, we have tapped some barrels ready."

"Sounds exciting." Bridget replied

"We have got the ram roast set up too and ready to go. Les will be in charge of that."

Ben stayed on the bar stool for a couple of pints chatting up Bridget. He was lierally drooling in his pint, thinking of getting off with her at the dance. Bridget caught him starring at her, but she tried to keep herself busy by serving other customers. Ben cleared off to the Loo.

"That lads got the hots for you!" Peter one of the locals commented.

"He is fun, but I am not that keen." replied Bridget

"Give him a try, you could move up to that lovely farmhouse he owns."

Bridget laughed the comment off.

It was the night of the Young Farmers dance and Ben was doing his final checks before heading off for a shower. He checked on the band, the disco and Les who was cooking the ram roast.

"That's smelling good." Ben mentioned to Les
"Proper Job, will be ready in about an hour, will let you be the first to taste it." Les loved doing ram roasts and was very good at cooking the meat, which was always succulent and tasty.

"It smells good Les, can't wait to have a taste, it's making me very hungry!" Ben had been working all day and had hardly any time to stop for food.

"I am just off for a shower and change Les, and will be down in half hour."

"It should be ready in an hour, so no hurry." Les replied

Ben rushed off to jump in the shower. He wanted to look his best for Bridget. He was convinced tonight would be the night to finally have a dance with her and show Bridget how he felt. Ben used Safari shower gel, he shaved and used plenty of deodorant too. He then threw on a clean pair of Levis which he placed his best leather belt on, and a crisp white shirt which made him feel fresh. He checked out his looks in the mirror whilst adding a bit of hair gel through his hair. Ben then bounced his way out of the house.

Ben's mum Margaret caught him running down the stairs.

"Hello Ben, you have scrubbed up well, who is the lucky lady?"

"It is Bridget, the farrier girl who works part time at the pub. I think she is the one mum."

"Good luck son, I look forward to meeting her."

Ben's mum was in her late seventies, and getting very frail. She wouldn't be going to the party, but Ben hoped he would bring back a potential wife for her to meet soon.

The guests started to flock into the marquee, young farmers and their friends from all over Devon. The band had started to set up. Mad Dog Macrea had a huge following, they were a talented English folk band, there was no doubt that they would get the crowd dancing with their infectious music.

"Here, taste this." Les offered Ben a slither of juicy lamb.

"Wow, that is fabulous." Ben was famished and the meat was very tasty.

"Well done Les."

Ben checked with the disco guy that he was happy, and the music was playing in a build up to the band. There were eight people serving behind the bar, six girls and two lads. Most were young farmer members, but also Bridget. It was the Hungry Horse that has supplied the beer for the night, and Tony the landlord had come along too to help.

Ben caught Bridget's eye

"Pint of Guinness please Bridget."

"Ok, lovely place you have here Ben."

"Thank you, yes it is a lovely place to live. I will be taking the place over from my father soon."

"You are a lucky chap, but it must be hard work on the farm to keep all this running."

"Yes, thanks for the drink, would you like one Bridget?" Ben asked

I will have half of larger with you Ben please." Bridget was getting thirsty already behind the bar.

The band were playing their set. The place was buzzing with most of the crowd on their feet bopping away. Bridget was very busy behind the bar; Ben was unable to chat her up.

*I will ask her for a dance once the disco starts up.* Ben thought, and he planned to get the DJ to put on a record for them. He asked for Robbie Williams '*She's The One.*'

Once the band stopped Ben made eyes at the DJ who was primed to put the Robbie Williams track on. Ben went over to the bar to find Bridget.

"Where is Bridget?" he asked one of the other barmaids.

"She's gone to the toilets I think?" was the reply

Ben decided to go and find her, to surprise her with his invitation for a dance to his chosen track. He walked out of the marquee and around the corner to the toilets. He stopped in his tracks. To his amazement and despair he found Bridget snogging another woman!

Ben couldn't believe his eyes. He was devastated. Bridget looked up and could see the disappointment on Ben's face.

"I am so sorry Ben, but I prefer women."

Ben ran off towards the house. He thought Bridget was the one, but Devon boy Ben got it so wrong as Bridget was batting from the other side.

# Should It Happen To A Barmaid?

## *Sixteen*

The Hungry Horse pub would often supply bars for various parties and functions. Tony the landlord had asked Bridget if she was free to help at a garden party, which was to be held on the coming Saturday night.

"Yes no problem, where is the house?" Bridget inquired

"It's at one of the beautiful properties overlooking Burgh Island nr Bigbury." Replied Tony

"That's fine, what time?"

"Garden party starts at 2pm, and carries on until about 10pm."

"Ok, shall I come to the pub first?"

"Yes, you can follow us there if you like, or travel with us, whichever you prefer."

"What's the celebration?" Bridget knew the location was a stunning one, so must be a good reason to hire in a marquee, caterers and outside bar.

Tony explained "It is a 50th wedding anniversary, for the author and crime writer Audrey Blake."

"I have heard of her, she writes thrilling books, how exciting, great I will look forward to helping out on that job." replied Bridget.

Tony was right. The location was stunning, helped by a beautiful clear day. Burgh Island was stood out to sea in all her majestic presence. The view from the marquee offered a superb focal point of the island which was breathtaking. The gardens were fantastic too. With interesting borders, shrubs and pots that any keen gardener would get excited about. Apparently Audrey Blake did most of the up keep of the garden herself.

"What a fab place!" Bridget said to Tony as they rocked up at the location for the party. Bridget helped Tony unload the booze and glasses for the party. Tony had come along the day before to tap the barrel, whilst most of the boxes were boxes and boxes of the finest champagne bottles. Tony had ordered the champagne in especially for the party from his wine suppliers.

"Will you be ok looking after the champagne please Bridget?"

"Yes of course Tony, I find it a great way of meeting people by topping up their glasses."

Bridget couldn't help looking up every now and then to take in the stunning location and views over the sea to Burgh Island. The Island has its own tractor to transport people from the beach. When the tide is in the Island can only be accessed this way or by boat. When the tide is out it is possible to walk over to the island. Apart from being a beautiful tiny island, it hosts a Hotel and a pub, namely the Pilchard Inn. *What a great way to spend an afternoon and evening, and be paid for it!* Bridget thought.

Bridget then caught sight of an older lady giving some young chap a hard time.

"No not there young man, put the pots either side of the entrance door!."

Bridget soon twigged that it was Audrey giving her young gardener assistant some grief as to where she wanted the finishing touches. She walked over where Tony was to ask if it was the famous Audrey Blake.

"Yes that's her." Tony chuckled

With that she headed over to the bar.

"Let me see what champagne you have bought along for us Tony."

"I have bought along some Dom Perignon 2004 Moet. Will that do?"

"It will have to if that is all you have bought along young man!"

Tony replied "I am sure your guests will be bowled over with the location Madam, they will enjoy the Champagne too."

Audrey strutted off in the other direction to nag one of

the chaps in charge of the string quartet bands.

"She is a bit of a dragon!" Bridget pointed out to Tony.

"No she is harmless really. A very shrewd lady who knows what she wants and gets it!" Tony had provided bars for functions of Audrey's before, and knew she was harmless and paid well.

The guests started to flood in. Most of the men were suited and the ladies wearing stunning outfits that made them look if they had just walked out of the summer edition of vogue magazine, and they probably had!

Bridget was doing her good champagne waitress job. Keeping an eye on the glasses, which people were holding, and topping them up when appropriate. She then caught her first glimpse of Jessica, Audrey's daughter. Jessica was in her thirties, and to Bridget she looked like an angel. Jessica also gave Bridget some very positive looks and feedback.

When Bridget went to top up Jessica's glass, Jessica flirted with Bridget, held her gaze and asked her some leading questions.
Introducing herself Jessica asked Bridget " Are you local? I haven't seen you at any of Mummy's parties before?"

Bridget replied, "No I am working part time at the Hungry Horse Pub, and am helping out Tony today with this event."

"Well my lovely, do come back and fill my glass some more!" teased Jessica

Bridget didn't dwell too long around Jessica, but needed to get away to gather her thoughts and clear her head. *Did I just hear that? Does Jessica know that I prefer Women under the sheets to men?* Bridget thought.

Bridget had felt really bad that she had given the wrong impression to Ben. It had taken him months to even set foot in the pub again. But yes, she did prefer the company of a female. She worked the marquee, kept the guests happy, and enjoyed banter with both the women and chaps at the party. She did do a fly by Jessica, Bridget couldn't help herself, and she was immediately attracted to Jessica's tall blonde leggy figure, and found it hard to believe that maybe Jessica preferred the company of women too. The flirting that Jessica was doing definitely suggested that.

Bridget found Tony, where he was chatting away to some chap about the beer barrels that were on offer.

"Tony please tell me who is Jessica? Where is she from?" Bridget asked.

"Oh trust you to pick up on that vibe Bridget. Jessica is from London, a fashion designer I believe, and yes, you have guessed it, she prefers women to chaps!"

"I thought so, she has been really flirty."

"She would be, as I understand she has recently split up

from her girlfriend. Be careful with that one, she has the same genes as her mother!"

"Oh ok, very scary then! She is very flirty." replied Bridget

Bridget found Jessica mesmerising.

Many of the guests were getting very merry. There had been a sit down luncheon, where Bridget had kept the champagne and wine glasses topped up. Jessica had been sitting on a table mainly full of chaps. They were giving her plenty of attention, but Jessica's attentions were towards Bridget.

One of the chaps on her table blurted out "Come on Jess, haven't found your soul mate yet?"

"No not yet, but you know me, none of you guys turn me on!!" Bridget replied

"You just don't give us a chance Jess!" the chap replied

Bridget heard all of this going on, she looked over to Jessica and smiled. Jessica smiled too and then gave Bridget a nod to the garden. Bridget was just about to renew her bottle of champagne for a full one. It was getting late, and there were a couple of bottles left that she had been dishing out after the cheese and coffee. *Jessica must be having a laugh?* Bridget thought.

Bridget spotted Jessica get up and leave the room, heading towards the toilets. Again Jessica looked for Bridget and hinted at her to head off out of the room. This time Bridget followed.

Bridget had a bottle of Champagne in her hand, Jessica picked up two glasses on her way out of the marquee.

"Let's go to the summer house." Jessica invited Bridget.

"Ok I will follow." Bridget was giggling, she had just had a very long day at work, and a little light relief to her was a bonus.

"In here." Jessica led Bridget into the summer house and left the door open. The view was amazing, with Burgh Island set in the moonlight with the lights twinkling in the dark.

"Now it's my turn to pour you a drink you lovely lady."

"Thank you, yes I need that. It has been a long day. "replied Bridget

"I absolutely love this spot, it is a view in a million." Jessica was on a high.

"Yes it certainly is just that." *It's the best location I have ever seen for a summerhouse.* Thought Bridget.

Jessica toasted the evening with Bridget. " Here's to stunning views, and to enjoying life!"

"I will drink to that." replied Bridget as she took a sip out of the champagne flute, whilst holding Jessica's gaze.

The girls enjoyed each other's company. They enjoyed the time together. Holding hands, kissing, caressing, and exploring each other's bodies.

"I better be getting back. Tony will be wondering where I am." Bridget was starting to feel uncomfortable.

"Yes mother will be seeking me out too, that's if she is not comatosed already!" Jessica giggled.

"Let's swop numbers" Jessica added I guess you are not in London that often, but it would be good to catch up again.
"Yes that would be nice. No I haven't many horses to shoe in London yet, but I could always get a job with the Royal Cavalry." Bridget laughed.

The girls had enjoyed the evening and were intrigued by each other, but maybe they would just remain friends.

# 'Should It Happen To A Barmaid?'

## *Seventeen*

The bars at the racecourse were buzzing. Lisa had taken on a job working at the local racecourse track, in one of the many licensed bars that are open there on race days.

Summer jumping is a thrilling way to spend an afternoon or evening, watching the National Hunt racehorses. These horses are trained by the top National Hunt trainers throughout the country, and ridden by many of the top jockeys. There is some thrilling racing on offer, and the day wouldn't be complete without the hospitality available too.

Lisa would work on rotation in the bars. There are bars that offer access to all televised races throughout the country for that day. Also greyhound racing is televised too. Along with on course betting shop and bookies for all to enjoy a flutter on their favourite bet if they wish to add to the occasion.

The other bars at the course are the restaurant, for those wishing to luncheon out before and during the races. The Silks bar, which offers fine wine champagne and cakes. The Owner and Trainers bar is popular with connections of the racehorses on the day.

Lisa was working this day in the William Hill bar. She had become familiar with the regular racing crowd, and would know what each of her regulars would like to drink. She would also discuss racing with them. The early birds would be trying to work out their Jackpot Totes or Placepot Totes for the day. They needed to pick out a winning or placed horse in every race. The punters would be thinking out loud and bouncing ideas off of her. She would be shrewd and try to keep her opinions and tips too herself. Lisa wouldn't want to sway their choice either way, just in case it was a deciding factor if they won or lost.

"Have you sussed out the winners then Jake?" Lisa asked one of the regular lads.

"Yes, I am going to scoop the Jackpot today!" Jake replied gleaming.

Lisa had heard it all before, but it can happen, so she is careful not to put a dampener on Jake's or anyone's enthusiasm.

"Good luck Jake, you deserve to be very lucky." Lisa had a bit of a soft spot for Jake, she had only met him through racing. Lisa knew that he was a keen racegoer, he enjoyed a pint or two, and also enjoyed following the sport, he often picked winners out. Jake was single, he spent many of his holidays from his trainee Solicitor job at the races. He was an intelligent lad. He had also ridden out for a few race yards, but struggling to make a lower weight he decided to follow his career path in Law.

"I am going to be very lucky today Lisa, I just have this hunch."
Lisa also worried that Jake would spend much of his

hard earned cash on having a flutter. She would see many racegoers either celebrating a win, or drowning their sorrows, and being fond of Jake, she wished him to be a winner, and felt for him if he lost.

"No friends with you today Jake?" Lisa asked whilst pulling his pint.

"The lads couldn't get the time off work today; I had put my holiday in months ago. The bosses at work scorn upon me liking racing, but I love it!

Lisa knew that Jake loved the thrill of racing, he loved being able to order a pint, to relax, to pick out a few winners, to watch the beautiful horses parade around the paddock, and to watch his bet of the day either come in first or trail in last. As long as they came home safe, it was all that Jake wished for. But could he crack the Tote and pick out the straight six winners for the Jackpot. Something that can be every race goers dream.

"What horses have you chosen today then Jake?" Lisa occasionally backed Jakes tips, as he did seem to pick out a few winners. The Tote bookies was situated opposite the bar, and the bar team would send a runner to put on the tips. As far as they were concerned it was legal, else they wouldn't be doing the bar job in the first place if they were not interested in racing.

"I have gone for 'Danehill Dancer' in the first, 'Absolute Darling' in the second, 'Tonto' in the third, 'Rocket Science' in the fourth, 'Critical' in the fifth and my choice for the sixth race is 'I've Said It'. I know you will not blurt my tips out to anyone Lisa, but having studied the form, I think they could all come close. I have done the Jackpot which is here today for £100,000 and the place pot separately for less than that. It only cost me two x £2 each bet.

"Good luck Jake I hope they win for you. If you win the Jackpot will you take me on holiday?"

"Yes of course Lisa, I enjoy coming here and the banter with you is cool, you are like my big sister should be, that's if I had one!"

Jake ordered another pint of Larger and supped some of it before heading out to watch the first race.

They set off at a strong pace, but Jake had no worries as 'Danehill Dancer' won by six lengths.

"Jake tipped that one, he is lucky, I should have put a bet on at 6-1." Lisa commented to Elly one of the other Barmaids.

Jake bounded back up to the bar.

"Another Larger please Lisa."

"Yes of course, that was a good win, did you back it as well as having it in your Jackpot?"

"I did!" Jake said jubilantly.

Jake's next horse to run was 'Absolute Darling', trained

by one of the local trainers Mike Hillier.

'Absolute Darling' was second favourite at 3-1. With the favourite horse for the race being odds on. Meaning that the bookies thought the favourite to be a certainty. But favourites are not always the winners. 'Absolute Darling' had every chance, the race being a three mile hurdle race and the horse was known to stay on forever in any going. 'Absolute Darling's' odds were 9-2.

Lisa thought she would give a fiver to the bar runner for her bet. She loved the name 'Absolute Darling', and knowing Jake did his form homework, thought the horse had a chance.

Jake supped his pint and went out to watch the race. Lisa could see the race from the screen monitors, and as most of the drinkers in the bar were watching the race, she could watch too. 'Absolute Darlin'g won by two lengths, with the favourite trailing home in fourth.

Jake touched base back at the bar with Lisa.

"Hey another winner Jake, thank you I backed that one!"

Jake had left his Larger behind the bar, he had only downed a third of his last pint, and Lisa would keep it behind the bar for him. Although he wasn't driving, he still liked to pace himself on drinking.

Next up was 'Tonto', trained by champion trainer Nigel Parker, 'Tonto' was a worthy favourite. Having won at the track before, he was Jake's banker and a certainty of the day. 'Tonto' was sent off odds on in the betting ring, he was something of a two mile hurdle race specialist. Every horse is allowed an off day or two in their career. But this day 'Tonto' came up trumps and won by ten lengths. The yard's team had come up trumps again!.

Jake bounced back into the bar.

"I am on a roll, I know this will be the day for me!" He grinned at Lisa

"Here is your drink. Shame I missed backing that one. Think I will follow you for the next though!" Lisa exclaimed, seeing that Jake was flying.

'Tight Screw' was Jake's next gamble. Trained by local trainer Justin Time, 'Tight Screw' had also been a previous course winner. He was owned by the Justin Time Race Syndicate. He had a couple of bad runs, so needed to come back to his best form to win here. 'Tight Screw' was 2-1 joint favourite, with one of the Welsh raiders 'Krazy Kat'.

Lisa put another fiver on 'Tight Screw' and thought she would be doing well if he won. He did exactly that, and fought a good battle with 'Krazy Kat', 'Tight Screw' went on to win by a length.
By now Jake was needing another Larger. Four down and two to go. What a dream it would be if he won the Jackpot!

'Critical' was the next horse on Jake's pick of six for the Jackpot. He had taken a risk on the mare who was claiming a mare's allowance in a race with eight geldings. He thought that her form looked good, and at the weights she should go close. But for some reason she was the outsider of the field at 33-1.

"It is all going to go pear shaped now Lisa. I fancy the mare's chances, but I think she will struggle to win."

"Well I am game for a fiver." replied Lisa "You have been lucky so far, so I am reinvesting my winnings, I have nothing to lose."

Jake finished his pint. He was starting to get nervous. If he did manage to win the Jackpot it would be more than enough to fund his college course, and give him a good start in life. He could even afford a share in his own racehorse, something that he could only ever dream about.

'Critical' was in second coming down the home straight, Jake's heart was sinking. *Maybe I could be in line for the placepot if 'Critical' is second?* Jake thought. The placepot also paid out well, but he would probably only end up with a few thousand shared out among many punters.

The horse leading then made an error and stepped at the last fence and the jockey got un- seated. This left 'Critical' with a clear lead and she won by a distance.

Lisa was beside herself a 33-1 winner and with a fiver on, she collected £170.

Jake waltzed into the bar.

"Did you like that one then Lisa?"

"Yes thank you so much, wicked, but how about you? So close to a jackpot?"

"Not sure I can go out and watch this race! It won't happen to me it never does."

By now Jake was attracting much attention in the bar area. Several punters wanted to know what his last bet of the day was. They had seen him jubilant, and Lisa too was excited, the atmosphere was starting to get infectious.

"Why have you chosen that horse?" asked one of the punters

"Local trainer, local track, trainer could have a double on the day, and Justin's son Henry is riding too, he rides the horse every day, so if anyone knows him Henry would get the best tune out of him."

There was a muttering around the room.

"Logical thought, good luck Jake, please take me on holiday if he wins!" Lisa has just poured Jake another pint, although he could hardly take a sip, he was that nervous.

"I will take you wherever you want to go Lisa, but knowing my luck he won't win!"

'I've Said It', was priced at 7-1, he was third favourite, and there were only seven in the race. Jake needed him to come in the first two to win a share of the placepot fund. If he won, then the jackpot was Jake's. Jake watched from inside the bar on one of the screens. Lisa had put her normal fiver on the horse too. She was quids in with the other bets, but so longed for Jake to realise his dream. The racecourse had also been tipped off that someone at their track was in line for the jackpot. The security guys with their walkie talkies were scouring the crowd looking for the likely candidate to tip off the TV screens.

Jake looked towards Lisa and put his hands up with his fingers crossed. She too did the same and gave him a beaming smile of support.

'I've Said It', was given a patient race by young Henry Time, he stalked the leaders and made his move down the home straight, having been headed over the last fence, but the combination fought back. The crowd roared the local horse and rider home and they won by two lengths.

Jake had been watching on the screen, he couldn't stand still. He was bouncing between the bar and where the TV moniter was. Lisa had laughed at the sight of him jigging about willing the horse home. Then Jake fainted. *Oh My God!* Lisa thought. She ran out from behind the bar. She alerted another barmaid to get the ambulance crew as soon as possible.

"Go quick, poor lad has fainted; he has just won £100,000!"

Not only were the Ambulance crew there, who were on the track anyway, but also the T.V and course presenters ready to interview Jake.

Jake came round, and he looked at Lisa.

"Where are we going on holiday then Lisa?"

# Should It Happen To A Barmaid?

## *Eighteen*

The six barmaids had met at a beer festival. Gemma, Nicky, Mandy, Julie, Lisa and Bridget had all found that they came from the same area in South Devon.

"How about we all go on summer holiday together? Gemma suggested.

"Why not?" replied Julie

"Where do you have in mind?" asked Nicky

"There is a great golfing resort in La Manga in Spain, we could go there, nice Villas with pools, and fun bars, well, so I hear?" suggested Gemma

"Let's do it!" added Mandy.

Bridget and Lisa were both a little reserved about the idea.

"I still have holiday left to take." Piped up Julie.

Bridget and Lisa both agreed, and came round to the idea.

The flights were soon booked and the ladies were heading off to La Manga in Spain. They had agreed to meet in the departure lounge at Bristol airport at 2pm, with the flight scheduled to take off at 1600 hrs.

"It will give us an hour or so to catch up before we head off, we can have a couple of large Gin and Tonic's before take-off." Gemma was the holiday organiser, and had asked Nicky to relay the info to the other lasses.

The girls soon realised that there were going to be plenty of single blokes on the holiday. Much of the departure lounge was filled up with sporty looking chaps. Ranging from early twenties, to early seventies in age. Once on the plane, it seemed to be Gemma that was attracting much of the male attention. There was one chap in particular that made a b-line for her.

"Hi my name is Ashley, and who are you lovely ladies?"

Gemma blushed and replied "Hi, I am Gemma, and these are my lovely new found friends and colleagues, Nicky, Lisa, Julie, Bridget and Mandy."

"Good to meet you." Ashley was beaming; he was like a child in a sweet shop that was so full of treats he didn't know which to look at or to choose first.

"I am here with my friends too." Ashley turned towards the chaps sat in their seats beside and in the seats behind him.
"May I introduce Patrick, Adam, Jeremy, Pete, and Chris."

The girls giggled

"Where are you lovely ladies heading to?" Pete asked

"La Manga." Piped up Nicky

"So are we, what a coincidence." Adam grinned

"Have you been there before?" Asked Pete

"No, it is our first trip out to Spain and our first trip anywhere as friends." Bridget piped up.

"We can show you around for the first night if you like? We will be out on the golf course during the day, and plan to head into town for supper and drinks after." Ashley seemed keen to get to know the girls more.

"That would be great, thank you." Gemma spoke for the girls and they all agreed.

On landing, the groups exchanged telephone numbers. Ashley and his friends were staying just two hotels away from where Gemma and the girls were staying. They agreed to meet up the following evening, for a night out at a restaurant followed by a pub crawl after.

The girls piled into a mini bus and headed off to their hotel, the Plaza. As they were climbing on board the bus, the chaps shouted out.

"Looking forward to tomorrow ladies?"

The girls waved as they loaded onto the minibus.

"Should we go?" Inquired Lisa

"Why shouldn't we? They look like a decent bunch of chaps, and they will know the best bars to direct us too."

Julie sounded keen.

"We have nothing to lose, let's go and have some fun."
Gemma also thought the chaps seemed decent enough.

The girls were tired after their flight. They topped up on
a few Gin and Tonics in the bar, before enjoying some
Mediterranean food in the restaurant. Their apartment
had a balcony, where they enjoyed a catch up finding
more out about each other and the barmaid jobs they had
encountered, before hitting their beds at 11pm.

Understandably the girls had a decent lie in the morning.
Gemma was the first to rise at 8.30am, she went exploring
the view from the balcony, it was stunning. With views far
and wide, over the golf course which seemed to span for
miles. Below their balcony lay the huge hotel swimming
pool, looking blue and inviting. One lone swimmer
was doing the breast stroke quietly, with the ripples of
the water being the only sound coming from that area.
There were many sunbeds, which lay empty. Gemma
guessed that most of the guests would be in the restaurant
tucking into breakfasts.

The other lasses started to surface whilst Gemma was
taking a shower. They were soon wandering around semi
naked, Julie put on the kettle for a cup of tea or coffee
for her other apartment mates. Bridget and Mandy sat on
the balcony in their T-Shirts waiting for their turn in the
shower.

"What's the plan today then?" Gemma asked the others
as she surfaced from the shower.

"Let's have a lazy day and top up the tans by that lovely pool after breakfast. We are out later, so good opportunity to unwind first." Julie suggested.

"Good idea." Piped up Nicky

The girls all enjoyed a hearty breakfast and then found some loungers by the pool. There was a bar which served complimentary drinks at lunchtime, so they had no need to go anywhere in a hurry on their first day of relaxing.

Ashley phoned Gemma late afternoon.

"Hi Gemma, are you still up for meeting up tonight?"

After checking with the other girls, Gemma replied "Yes we are, where are you suggesting we meet?"

"Antonio's restaurant at 7pm, we have provisionally booked a table for twelve of us." Ashley was hoping the girls were still up for a night out.

"Yep we are all up for that, where is Antonio's?" Gemma asked

"It is only two streets away overlooking the beach, the Plaza will give you directions."

"Great we will see you at seven." Gemma turned to the others. "Game on, we are going to be shown the town tonight."

"Let's have a spa first before we get ready." Suggested Julie

They all agreed and headed off for a spa before getting themselves dressed up.

Gemma was first ready, she had chosen some music to put on whilst the others were getting their outfits and make-up sorted. She had packed some CD's in her luggage, and was pleased to find that the T.V in the hotel had a CD/DVD player too. Gemma chose a Bob Marley CD to get the girls in the party mood. They also had a couple of bottles of Prosseco which they had bought in duty free on their way over.

They headed off merrily to Antonio's restaurant to be greeted by the golfing chaps who were already there.

"Hi there lovely ladies, come and join us." Ashley was a bit of a gentleman, and having got up, he pulled a chair out for each of the ladies one by one.

The girls were lapping up the attention. Ashley definitely had the hots for Gemma, and she did find him attractive. All the girls were enjoying the attention, although Bridget seemed to be more interested in Mandy than the chaps!

The boys ordered some fine Rioja wine for the table, and the girls supped away.

The banter and flirting was flowing well, and Gemma had let on that they were all barmaids.

"So ladies, do tell us what barmaids get up to in their pubs then?" Pete led the questions.

"Plenty, we have great fun most of the time. It is a great way to meet people and socialise. We have also been known to get up to all sorts of naughtiness, the opportunities are endless." Gemma and the rest of the girls were in fits of giggles.

"We will have to get you a bit more tipsy so that you can give us a sample of what goes on." Chris looked as if could be a very naughty golfer.

"Well, we have a policy, that we definitely do not kiss and tell!" Mandy winked at Chris as she sipped her wine.

"That's what we like to hear." Chris said grinning. The chaps all agreed.

The group left the restaurant and headed for a guided tour of the town as the chaps had promised. The ladies all paid for their own food, with the chaps treating them to the wine.

After a short tour off the historic buildings, the chaps offered a choice of two nightclubs.

"We are guided by you chaps, so wherever you think has the funkiest music for us to have a good dance in." Gemma loved music and enjoyed dancing till midnight.

The club was buzzing, the girls bought the first drink round, to thank the chaps for buying the wine in the restaurant. They all then agreed on a kitty and put £20 in each.

Ashley and Chris danced with the girls, whilst Jeremy, Pete, Adam, and Patrick propped up the bar. Patrick was interested in the beautiful Spanish barmaid in the club, and looked to be trying his luck with her.

The kitty money was soon spent, and they all topped it up with another £20 each. This time they ordered a round of cocktail slammers.

"Twelve Tequila Slammers please?" Patrick asked the Spanish barmaid.

By now the ladies were getting well sozzled. They all downed the cocktails and went off for another dance. All the chaps joined in this time.

"One more for the road I think? Do you agree ladies?" Patrick was looking for any excuse to head back up to the bar to flirt with the beautiful barmaid.

"Can we have 'Long Slow Comfortable Screw Up Against The Wall' cocktails please? Asked Julie

All were in fits of laughter

Patrick was up at the bar like a shot requesting those cocktails from his dream Spanish barmaid.

Instead of heading back to the dance floor, Ashley and Gemma snuck off leaving the club.

"I will walk you back to the hotel, and show you the golf course on the way." Ashley had hold of Gemma's hand

and squeezed it gently.

Gemma, like the other barmaids could hold her drink. She was very merry, but in control. They had been drinking over a space of five hours, with plenty of energetic dancing in-between. Ashley led Gemma to the golf course, the couple were laughing and giggling. It was a beautifully clear night, and the stars were shining in the moonlit sky.

"What's that shed over there?" teased Gemma

"It's the groundsmans hut." Replied Ashley

"Let's sneak in there." Gemma seemed keen.

Ashley tried the door and it was open. Once inside the couple starting kissing and cuddling.

"How about that 'Long Slow Comfortable Screw Up Against The Wall' for real? Ashley whispered.

And within seconds that's exactly what happened to Gemma.

Meanwhile back at the Club, Bridget was trying to get off with Mandy, however Mandy had other ideas and had fallen for Chris.

"Come on Mandy, I will walk you back to your hotel." Chris led Mandy off.

He went to give Mandy a kiss at the hotel door, but Mandy grabbed his hand and led him into the lift.

The girls' apartment was on the fifth floor. Once in the lift the couple started a passionate kiss. The lift was full of mirrors on all sides. They were both turned on by the sight of each other getting passionate in the lift. Once up on the fifth floor, Chris pushed the ground floor button again. Mandy was in fits of laughter. They travelled up and down the lift until they had both become so excited they reached the heaven button together. Fortunately there were two lifts, but as they came out of the lift they saw Bridget coming out of the next door lift. She had walked home alone as Patrick had stayed trying his luck with the Spanish barmaid, and she had probably followed Mandy and Chris home.

Mandy invited Chris in for a coffee before he headed back to his own hotel. Bridget went straight to her room and crashed out sulking.

Jeremy and Lisa were the next through the apartment door. Jeremy and Lisa had gone for a walk and had found a park bench to sit on. They had had a good chat. Lisa was totally in love with her chap back home. The officer, Edward Gold, who had interviewed her for the Naval bar job. They had been together for over a year now. She was determined not to cheat on him, even if they were girls on tour. Jeremy agreed he too had a lovely devoted wife at home, and he too was of the same mind set as Lisa.

Pete and Julie had also headed to the golf course. They managed to find a comfortable bunker, and had sat looking at the stars, before writing silly things in the sand. Hopefully the groundsman would tidy the bunker up before the golfers were out on the course in the morning. The couple had incredible fun in the sand.

"Mmmmm hole in one!" Pete said as they enjoyed reaching fulfilment together. He added "That's the first time I have bonked in a bunker!"

Adam and Nicky had headed back to the lads' apartment, knowing that the others had headed off in difference directions. Adam grabbed a bottle of Champers out of the fridge and led Nicky into his room. Adam was very fit, he had an eight pack that had Nicky melting into his arms. They had fun between the sheets, after which they fell asleep with Adam's arms around Nicky's waist. Nicky left the hotel room in the morning and had her walk of shame in her party dress back to her hotel. Adam had already left for his round of golf. The girls cheered her back in the door.

Gemma and Ashley were both too drunk to have much fun that night. However, they more than made up for it on the flight home though. Ashley had given Gemma the nod, and both headed off to the toilet at the same time. They managed to sneak in the toilet together. It was their last chance to catch up. After the first night out, the groups had stayed apart. An occasional text had been all the contact they had, apart from some friendly light chat in the bars.

Gemma had her back up against the wall. They were both turned on, not just by the mission of joining the five mile high club, but by each other's sexuality. They had fancied each other from the moment they met on the flight over.

Ashley was well aroused and had no trouble giving his all to Gemma. She too found it easy to let herself go. She too found it easy to let herself go, the perfect end to a perfect holiday.

The End